HIDDEN TRAILS

LEIF J. ERICKSON

TABLE OF CONTENT

Chapter 1

I stood on the edge of wonder. What lies ahead in the mythical dreams of the forest? Who might we find as we explore her secrets? Stories tell us of witches and warlocks, fairies and imps, trolls and unicorns, or maybe just of ourselves. The fog surrounds us; the symphony of nature envelops our ears. We find what our hearts truly desire. We hear, but we don't listen. We fear what the lyrics might say. The trees are skyscrapers; the grass, asphalt; and the rustling of leaves is the sound of their rush hour.

What do we find walking her paths and admiring her beauty? We find in ourselves the basic need to connect— to our environment, our surroundings, and to those whom we love. People who run from you cannot handle the fear of losing connections. They live in the moment, ultimately alone no matter how many people they surround themselves with. Those who choose to embrace, to connect, find a friend in the forest and in their lives. They are never truly alone.

The spring air was warm with the promise of a new season bringing forth warmth and beauty. All the plants on the state college campus were vibrantly green and blossoming. Animals returned from hibernation and explored the new season in the evening hours. The students, like animals shedding their winter fur, shed their coats and hurried around campus in tank tops and shorts.

In a rowdy bar and grill near campus, three senior guys sat on an outdoor patio, enjoying burgers and a pitcher of beer. The guys ate quickly, as if they were on a mission to devour the beef and fries before anyone else could. They kept their eyes open, waiting for someone to join them. At a glance, it would be hard to tell the guys apart. They were all muscular, frat boys with gelled, spiky hair, fake tans, and wearing cargo shorts with polo shirts.

They didn't put their burgers down until two stunning women walked up to them and sat down. One, Heidi, was very petite, black, and wore her short black hair in a ponytail. Her jean shorts and university t-shirt fit her well. The other woman, Roxy, was tall and thin, with silky, shiny, brown hair that cascaded down her back. Roxy was tan and fashionable, preferring designer labels and matching her makeup to her accessories. Before they could say anything to the guys, a waitress rushed up to the table.

"Roxy, Heidi," the waitress said in a bubbly voice. "What can I get ya?"

"Another pitcher of beer," the only guy with glasses said. "And glasses for both."

"Only one glass," Roxy said. "I'll have a Gray Goose martini."

"Sounds good," the waitress said walking away.

"No beer tonight?" the glasses guy asked.

"Please Mike," Roxy scoffed. "I never drink beer."

"Can't blame me for trying," Mike said. "I thought Todd here was going to drink that pitcher by himself."

"It's hot out," Todd said with a mouth full of burger. "Have to stay hydrated."

"Gross," Heidi said. "Steve, where's Greg? I thought you two were going to be working on that project earlier."

"He needed to stay at the library for something. Where's the rest of your crew?"

"Jennifer and Leah are on their way," Heidi smiled. "They were in the labs. Savannah was at the gym."

As Heidi finished speaking, two more women walked up to the table and sat down. Leah, tall and muscular, but a little thick, wore her red hair cropped short. Jennifer, a hauntingly beautiful blonde bombshell, was shorter than Leah, but had a powerful presence with piercing blue eyes. Jennifer kissed Mike before sitting down.

"Love you babe," Mike said.

"Love you too," Jennifer said.

"You guys eat?" Mike asked.

"We did earlier," Jennifer said. "We've been in the lab."

"You wore that to the lab?" Todd asked, referring to her black business ensemble.

"I put a lab coat over it," Jennifer said. "I had an interview earlier."

"How'd it go?" Mike asked.

"The same as all the others," Jennifer said. "Long, lots of hard questions. My God, the job market is competitive right now. I can barely get my foot in the door. Just getting an interview is like pulling teeth."

"I know the feeling," Todd said. "I've interviewed at ten different companies since January and I haven't gotten any callbacks."

"I've took the offer I got," Mike said, "but it's a jerk-off job. I took it so I would at least have some money coming in while I looked for something better."

"And so we can pay for some of the wedding," Jennifer said with a smile.

"Your dad was pushy about that," Mike said. "He said I needed something. The wedding's a month away so I took it."

"He's proud of you," Jennifer said kissing Mike. "I am too."

"Thank you," Mike said. "Heidi, what about you?"

"I'm going to work as a secretary for my older brothers," Heidi said. "Two of them started a business together."

"I thought you guys didn't get along," Steve said.

"I don't," Heidi said. "But there are bills to pay."

"How's that gonna work?" Mike asked. "I remember some of the stories you told about growing up with them, you sure you can work with them?"

"Their secretary just had twins and wants to take a three year leave," Heidi said. "I'm there to get some experience and show that I can handle a job. It's only three years with them...but it will be a long three years. The market should be better when I'm done there."

"I barely got into grad school," Roxy said. "There's so many people applying right now; it's very competitive."

"Please, they took one look at your dad's checkbook and rolled out the red carpet for you," Todd said. "I've always wondered why you went to a state school. You've got straight A's and a multi-millionaire father. Why?"

"To be close to my dad," Roxy said. "Ever since mom left, he depends on me."

"Like what?" Todd asked.

"I buy his clothes," Roxy said. "Give him advice on what he should wear for big business meetings, making sure he's eating right, stuff like that."

"Whatever," Todd said. "Steve, I know you're in the same boat as me."

"Right," Steve said. "No idea what I'm going to do in a couple weeks when we graduate from this place."

"It's a beautiful Thursday," Mike said. "Perfect weather, perfect friends, let's just enjoy it. This could be the last time we are all here."

Mike's words sunk in around the table. This was the last couple of weeks of college. Soon, they would be kicked out of the comforts of school and have to make their way in the real world. The waitress dropped off their drinks and took Leah and Jennifer's orders.

"I'm going full time at the state park," Leah said. "Maintaining trails and cleaning up after tourists. Why did I go to four years of school for this?"

"How's the pay?" Jennifer asked.

"Horrible," Leah said. "And what really sucks, I haven't had any time this year to hit the gym. I'm always working on school stuff. A business degree with an economics minor and I'm cleaning toilets. I feel horrible. I've gained weight, something like twenty pounds this year, lost a lot of my muscle mass and strength, and I have a useless degree."

"You'll have time for the gym though," Todd said.

"Only because I got a part-time job at one," Leah said. "It doesn't pay very well, but I get a free membership. I need to work two jobs just to make it. I wish I didn't have to grow up."

"I think we all wish that," Heidi said. "School is so much easier than the real world."

Mike was about to say something when Savannah approached. Savannah stood slightly over six feet tall with a very powerful, muscular body. She carried herself proudly, both dominant and authoritative. Everyone found her intimidating. Her curly blonde locks dropped past her broad shoulders complementing her blue eyes and fine features. She wore red running shorts, a white tank top, and sneakers; she looked like she'd just stepped out of the shower.

"What'd I miss?" Savannah asked as she poured herself a beer.

"That none of us are ready for the next couple of weeks," Jennifer said.

"I'm not too worried about it," Savannah said.

"You've got stuff lined up though, little miss accountant," Todd said.

"Don't call me that, Toddy" Savannah said. "It is what it is, I guess. The pay is good, but I have to wear business attire."

"There's nothing wrong with dressing up," Roxy said sipping her martini. "You really should dress up more often, Savannah. You always look like you are going to the gym."

"That's because she's always going to the gym," Todd laughed. "I mean, look at those arms. How much can you bench?"

"It's not going to be that bad," Savannah said ignoring Todd. "I just wish I could have a little more time here."

"We all wish that Savannah," Jennifer said. "None of us are ready to leave."

"I just wish that it could be like this more," Savannah said. "We're going to lose touch with each other."

"There is something called the Internet," Mike said. "And we won't be very far away."

Savannah was about to say something when Greg, a college frat boy who'd let himself go, excitedly rushed up to the group, panting and out of breath.

"You guys will never guess what I discovered," he said.

"Your feet?" Todd joked.

"A woman?" Savannah asked with a sly grin.

"No, you guys," Greg said. "I found it. I found what we've been looking for!"

"What's that?" Jennifer asked.

"The hidden trail," Greg said. The group fell silent.

"The hidden trails," Savannah broke the silence cautiously. "You're talking about the legend at Foothill State Forest? You mean the hidden trail somewhere in the woods that the rangers covered up and no one is allowed to walk anymore?"

"That's right," Greg said. "I found it. We need to hike it. You know how cool it would be? We need to get out there."

"We don't have time, Greg," Mike said. "We've got finals."

"Oh come on! Let's have one more big event before we cap off college," Greg said. "We've talked all semester about doing something and we've talked the last four years about hiking the hidden trails."

"We've been in that forest hundreds of times," Savannah said. "I started running the trails when I was thirteen; I've never seen any hidden trails there. They don't exist."

"But they do," Greg said taking a map from his backpack. "Look at this."

Greg set the map on the table. The map was of the state forest as it was 1890. There was a network of trails and logging camps. Greg took out a modern forest map and set it next to the old map. Greg pointed out where a trail on the older map and where it would be on the current one.

"This trail goes into the foothills," Greg said. "It stops at the base of the mountain. We should hike up there."

"I have so much work to do," Heidi said. "There's no way. I barely have time to be here right now."

"We need a bachelor party. The guys could go out and make sure it's safe. Then, after the wedding, we could all go out there. The first adventure of our new adult lives," Greg said.

"Being an adult is nothing to celebrate," Leah said.

"Agreed," everyone chimed in.

"We should do something though," Savannah said. "You look at our partying and playing it would be a damn shame for us to go out with a whimper. We need to shake it up."

"But we have so much work," Jennifer said.

"Then we'll go and see what there is out there," Mike said. "We'll leave tomorrow after class and come back on Sunday. After the wedding, we'll all go out there. You girls can party it up here tomorrow night."

"I don't know," Jennifer said. "We have so much wedding planning yet to do, Mike."

"Once school is done your sisters will help," Mike said. "I think we should do this."

"What the hell," Steve said. "I'm in."

"Why not?" Todd said.

"It's settled," Mike said. "Tomorrow after class the guys are hitting the hidden trails."

Chapter 2

It was a beautiful spring day and almost all the students were out and about, Frisbees and baseballs were sailing through the air. Runners took in that first good outdoor run, and even the students who were studying sat outside on the grass enjoying the air.

Almost all the students were outside, except for one group of girls who'd had a bit too much fun the night before. Inside Jennifer's apartment on the west edge of the campus, Jennifer and the girls were trying to sleep off their wild night. It had started at an upscale restaurant with $20 martinis, but the evening ended at a house party with keg beer.

Heidi was the first one to move, but that was only to rush to the bathroom. As she stumbled through the messy apartment, she tried to avoid stepping on anyone—most of the girls wound up crashing on the floor or in chairs. Heidi felt the room spin and tried to remember how their night had gotten so out of control. Heidi made it to the bathroom just in time. Jennifer woke up slightly confused as she stretched and tried not to wake Leah, who shared the sofa with her. She walked to the bathroom door.

"You okay?" Jennifer asked.

"Lovely," Heidi mumbled back before vomiting again.

"Need someone to hold your hair?" Jennifer asked.

"No," Heidi grunted.

Jennifer braced herself against the wall before shuffling to the counter where her cellphone was sitting. Jennifer called Mike's phone. She wasn't sure if he would have his phone on, or if he would be in location where there was reception, but she wanted to try. The phone rang several times before it went to voicemail.

"Hey honey, just wanted to check in and see what was going on. How's the trail? Give me a call when you get this. The girls and I will be studying today so call anytime. Love you."

Jennifer hung up and looked over toward her friends. They hadn't partied this hard since their freshman year in college. Savannah, laying on the floor without a blanket or pillow, stretched and opened her eyes.

"What time is it?" Savannah managed to ask.

"About ten," Jennifer said fiddling with her phone.

"That was a hell of a party," Savannah said. "I don't think I've ever drank that much. Nothing weird happened last night, did it? I don't remember much."

"Not that I remember," Jennifer said. "The booze just flowed."

Savannah was about to say something when Heidi stumbled out of the bathroom. She looked horrible, hair a mess, puffy bags under her eyes, flushed, and holding her stomach. She dragged herself over to a chair and fell into it.

"I'm never doing that again," Heidi said.

"Wasn't that bad," Leah said, cracking her eyes open. "You want to keep it down?"

"I think a few more hours would be good," Jennifer said slumping into an open chair.

Jennifer settled in and soon all the girls were fast asleep.

The sun had just set, but the campus was still a beehive of activity. The evening saw students out in full force enjoying weather—except for Jennifer and her friends. They were all back in Jennifer's apartment, worried that no one had heard from the boys.

Leah and Savannah sat at the table playing cards; Heidi was occupied with her phone; Roxy watched television as Jennifer paced around the room playing agitatedly on her phone as her thoughts were consumed with Mike. Jennifer had left six voicemails and a ton of text messages, but there was still no word from Mike or any of the other guys.

"Something went wrong," Jennifer said. "They should have answered us by now."

"Calm down," Leah said looking up from her card game and taking a drink from a flask. "I'm sure they're deep in the foothills right now. There's no reception up there."

"One of them should have walked out and called us," Jennifer said. "They should have gotten into contact with us. They were supposed to be home last night."

"The trails are probably longer than they thought," Savannah said. "I'm sure that's what happened to them. Try not to worry."

Jennifer was about to speak when her phone rang. She looked at the number and her face was flushed with excitement. The caller ID indicated that the call was coming from the Foothill State Park.

"It's from the park. I'll put it on speaker," Jennifer said as she answered the phone. The other women stopped what they were doing and gathered around. "Hello?"

"Jennifer? This is Ranger Lacey Mark," Lacey said through the phone. "How are you doing this evening?"

"A little nervous," Jennifer said, fear edging into her voice. "I've been waiting to hear from Mike and his friends. They were at the park this weekend."

"That's what I needed to talk to you about," Lacey said. "This weekend there was a retreat for teenaged girls at one of the campsites. A couple of them went missing so we went searching for them."

"What does this have to do with Mike and his friends?"

"While we were searching for the girls, we came across Mike's campsite. It was empty and it didn't look like it had been used that day. This was Saturday afternoon."

"Okay?" Jennifer asked.

"I just got back from the site," Lacey said. "All their gear is still there, but they haven't been back. Nothing's been moved from where it was on Saturday."

"What are you trying to say?" Jennifer asked.

"I'm sorry, Jennifer," Lacey said. "They're missing. Have heard from them?"

"No," Jennifer said. "I've left calls and messages, but they haven't responded. What do you think happened?"

"I don't know," Lacey said. "Did they say anything to you before they left? Were they going to try the rapids or go climbing? Anything dangerous?"

"No," Jennifer said. "It was going to be just hiking and camping. They would have alerted you if they were going to try something like that."

"Here's what we do next, I've noted that they are missing and if there's been no contact by tomorrow evening, then I will alert the police and file missing person reports. That's our standard procedure. I'm sorry I can't do more now, but we have to wait twenty-four hours. We'll search the area tomorrow and ask everyone if they've seen them. I'm sure they're safe. They've probably just gotten lost or stuck. Try not to worry."

"I won't," Jennifer said. "I know they wouldn't have gone somewhere dangerous without telling someone—maybe you're right and they are lost. Thanks for letting me know, Lacey. Have a good evening."

"You too, Jennifer," Lacey said with a hint of confusion in her voice.

"Goodbye," Jennifer said as she ended the call.

The apartment was silent for a moment. Everyone except Leah was frozen. Leah pulled a half full bottle of cheap vodka out of her bag and poured a good amount into her flask, put the bottle away, and took a large swig of her drink.

"You okay, Jennifer? You seem rather calm about all this."

"I'm not," Jennifer said. "We have a big problem."

"They're lost," Roxy said.

"They're not lost," Jennifer said. "Well, they might be, but more than that, they aren't where they are supposed to be. If they're found on the hidden trail, they might get in trouble. Plus, the rangers and police won't be looking on those trails."

"Then we just wait for them," Heidi said. "They will either call or return soon."

"No," Jennifer said. "They would have called by now."

"I know what you're thinking, Jennifer," Savannah said. "We have classes. It's the end of the semester, our futures are on the line here. We graduate in two weeks."

"And the guys need to be there to graduate with us," Jennifer said.

"Wait," Roxy asked, "what are we talking about here?"

"We're going to the park tomorrow," Jennifer said.

"But we have class, tests to study for, and final papers to write," Heidi said.

"And the guys have all those things to do too. If they are lost, we need to go out there and find them. They would do the same thing for us."

"No, they wouldn't," Savannah said. "Mike would for you, but Steve and Todd wouldn't be sober long enough to care. Greg might, but he would never be able to agree on a plan."

"Girls," Jennifer said, "this is my fiancée. We are getting married in a month. I have to have a groom for there to be wedding."

"She's right," Leah said. "We have to do this. They've saved us before. Remember spring break last year—"

"You don't need to remind us. We were all drunk and shit happened." Savannah sighed, "I hate to say it, but I agree with you. We need to be well supplied and ready for anything."

"Supplied?" Roxy said.

"GPS units, copies of the map Greg found, and food and water to start. We'll be doing a lot of hiking and it's been unusually warm. They're talking temperatures in the upper eighties and possibly ninety tomorrow so we need to dress and pack light. We need to move fast."

"Pack light?" Heidi asked. "How the hell long do you think we're going to be out there?"

"We're bringing tents," Savannah said. "I'm sure we'll have to spend the night."

"I can't miss that much class," Roxy said. "Not this late in the year."

"I'm going," Jennifer said. "Savannah, I gather that you're coming with, who else?"

"I will," Heidi said. "It's the right thing to do."

"Why the hell not?" Leah said taking another drink.

"I don't know," Roxy said.

"It's okay if you don't want to go, Roxy," Jennifer said. "I know that you aren't the biggest fan of the forest or hiking."

"I don't want to disappoint you guys," Roxy said. "I'll go, but I have to be back by Wednesday night."

"We'll take two cars," Jennifer said. "Roxy, you can leave Wednesday, but if we haven't found them by then I'm staying until we do." There was a silence in the room for a moment.

"What about the other thing Lacey said?" Savannah asked.

"What?" Jennifer said.

"Missing teenage girls?" Savannah said. "You don't think they found the guys?"

"They would never," Jennifer said. "Not with teenagers."

"Guys out camping, drinking a little," Savannah said. "Couple girls show up, fake names and ages given, Mike wouldn't, but the others might."

"Speaking from experience there, Savannah?" Heidi asked with a sly grin.

"Hell yeah," Savannah said. "I was fourteen."

"Fourteen!" Roxy exclaimed.

"We didn't go all the way," Savannah said. "I was at a volleyball workshop at a summer camp. I didn't want to be there. It was really lame and I was far and away the best player there."

"But you've always played soccer," Heidi said. "Why were you at a volleyball camp?"

"Parents," Savannah said shrugging. "They wanted a volleyball star. Well, technically they wanted all boys who were football and wrestling stars, but I was supposed to play volleyball, not soccer, because I'm a girl. The point is that I snuck out with a couple other girls. We met up with some college guys at a campsite, got some booze, whatever."

"They didn't question your age?" Heidi asked.

"I was five-eleven," Savannah said, "and already pretty muscular. I could pass for a college girl. We got drunk, they got blown, everyone was happy."

"And they say sports are supposed to keep girls away from drinking and sex," Heidi said.

"They say a lot of crap," Savannah said.

"Enough," Jennifer said. "The guys wouldn't have been with those girls. Even Todd would have more morals than that. We leave tomorrow at six and not a second later."

"Don't worry," Savannah said seriously. "We will find them. I promise you that."

Jennifer tossed and turned in her sleep, scenarios of what could have happened ran through her head. By the time she was able to sleep, her nerves were shot. She'd asked Savannah to stay the night, not wanting to be alone. Savannah had agreed, but it didn't help. At 4:30am, Jennifer's phone rang. She shot up and grabbed her phone; the caller id indicated that it was Mike's phone.

"Hello? Mike?" Jennifer asked frantically, waking up Savannah in the process. "Oh God, Mike, I've been so worried. What the hell happened?" Only static came across the line.

"Mike?" Jennifer was almost hysterical. "Mike, please..." Savannah stood up and went over to Jennifer, concerned.

"Mike!" Jennifer shouted.

"Don't..." Mike's voice barely came through the phone. "Don't...come."

"What?" Jennifer asked through her tears.

"Don't...walk...the...hidden...trail."

Suddenly, the call dropped. Jennifer was crying hysterically, not knowing what to do.

Savannah tried to calm her down, but nothing worked. Jennifer was beside herself.

"Jennifer," Savannah said hugging her friend, "don't jump to conclusions."

"No, Savannah," Jennifer said. "Get up, we're going now. Call the others, this rescue mission has to leave right now."

"Are you sure?"

"We have to go now," Jennifer said getting out of bed. "I won't lose Mike. I can't."

Chapter 3

A half hour after the sun broke over the horizon, two cars, a luxury sedan and a high-end SUV pulled into the ranger station at Foothill State Park. Two rangers, Morris Foss and Lacey Mark stood outside the station talking in hushed voices as five girls piled out of the cars. Morris's face lit up when he saw them, always having a slight crush on two of the girls.

"Come on, ladies," Jennifer said, "we have to get a move on."

"Calm down," Leah said taking a sip from her flask. "We have the whole day."

"The day might not be enough," Jennifer said sternly. The rangers approached them.

"I take it there hasn't been any word?" Ranger Foss asked.

"None," Jennifer said. "We're going out to look for them. They must have gotten lost somewhere in the forest. They wanted to hike high into the foothills."

"There's a lot of old trails up there," Ranger Mark said. "Some that aren't ours. Private trails and all."

"There's nothing dangerous up there, is there?" Roxy asked.

"Shouldn't be," Ranger Foss said. "The animals have been out of hibernation long enough that they're awake and fed. It's rare to get a bear or big cat in that area anyway."

"Are there people up there?" Roxy asked.

"No," Ranger Foss said, "nothing like that. Here's the deal, girls, the police will be here tomorrow morning to search and..."

"That's not a good idea," Savannah interrupted.

"Why not?" Ranger Mark asked.

"Lacey," Savannah put her arm around the ranger and escorted her away from the group, "come with me. I need to talk to you, woman to woman."

Savannah took Lacey past the cars and over to a patch of grass. Savannah positioned Lacey so they would be talking with their backs to the others.

"Can you keep a secret?" Savannah asked.

"Yes."

"We want to find those boys before any cop does."

"Why is that?" Lacey asked sternly.

"This was Mike's bachelor party," Savannah said making a smoking gesture with her hand. "Catch my drift? Having the police find them wouldn't make for the best way to end college and start their adult lives."

"That doesn't sound like adult behavior to me," Lacey said disappointedly. "Damn kids. I thought you guys were better than that. So, it that what you'd do when you come up here to camp? Get stoned and have an orgy?"

"Nothing like that, Lacey," Savannah said. "We've never done drugs up here before. This was a one-time thing for them because Mike and Jennifer are getting married."

"Yeah right," Lacey scoffed. "The beauty and wonder of this place and you use it as your party grounds. It's sad, you know? I thought you guys were more mature than that."

"Well, we're not," Savannah said. "One thing I've learned Lacey is that you need to get used to disappointment. It seems like that's all the worlds full of anyway."

"You girls have anything with you?" Lacey asked. "Be honest."

"I'm sure Leah has some booze," Savannah said. "She's been drinking non-stop lately. Other than that, we're just here to find our friends. I'm asking you, as a friend, hold the police back as long as you can, give us a chance to find them and kick their asses first."

"Okay," Lacey said. "On one condition."

"Name your price."

"Put in a good word for me with Todd," Lacey said with a sly grin. "He's such a fox."

"Done," Savannah said.

Savannah walked back to the group. They were in the process of checking over all the supplies and making sure that they'd brought everything they'd need. They made sure everything was packed light and easy to move. Everyone would have something to carry. Morris and Lacey watched as the women prepped. Morris couldn't help but notice that they were wearing sweatshirts and sweatpants, heavier clothing than the weather necessitated.

"I don't know if you girls checked the weather," he said, "but it's been unusually hot here. Yesterday was one of the hottest days on record for May and today looks to break that. You have plenty of sunscreen?"

"Yes, we do," Jennifer said.

"You're going to cook in those outfits," Ranger Foss said. "It may even hit triple digits."

"If you're trying to get us out of our clothes," Leah said. "You're not being very subtle."

"It's not that..." Ranger Foss tried to explain.

"We know," Leah said. "We're prepared."

As they finished getting ready, they stripped down to various styles of shorts and either swimming or athletic tops. The only girl that didn't have her stomach fully exposed was Roxy, who was wearing a designer swimsuit with a designer swimming skirt. The girls put their cover-ups in their backpacks and slung the packs onto their backs.

"We ready to go?" Jennifer asked.

"Hang on one second," Ranger Foss said rushing into the ranger station.

"What's he getting?" Savannah asked.

"Who knows?" Lacey replied. Before anyone could say anything else, Morris returned with a walkie-talkie in his hand. He handed it to Savannah.

"Take this," Ranger Foss said. "It has reception throughout the park. If you need anything, or if the guys need medical attention, use it."

"Reception throughout the park?" Savannah asked looking at the devise in her hand. "I thought these things were only good for a couple of miles."

"Normally," Ranger Foss replied. "But we have a number of repeater tower on the edges of the park. It's crystal clear anywhere in the park. Promise me that you will keep it on at all times.

The battery is charged and will last a few days on standby."

"We'll be careful, Morris," Savannah said. "Thank you. Come on, ladies, let's move."

The girls followed Savannah as she walked over a swell of land and out of sight towards the main trail entrances. Morris looked at his watch then filled out a form as to the time and date of arrival and placed it on the windshields of both cars. Lacey just watched as the girls walked away.

"What is it, Lacey?" Morris asked.

"Something that Savannah said to me," Lacey replied. "They don't want the police here."

"Why not?" Morris asked.

"She implied that the guys were partying and smoking weed. She said that if the police found them with drugs, then it would really hurt them professionally."

"Damn these little brats," Morris said shaking his head. "Why can't these kids grow up?"

"Who knows?" Lacey said. "But there was something else. I've known Savannah for a long time. She came here when she was in high school, running the trails for practice. I've ran with her before—we're friends."

"What are you getting at?" Morris asked.

"I don't think she was being totally honest with me," Lacey said. "I feel like there was some other reason that she didn't want the police to be out looking for them."

"What?"

"I may have an idea," Lacey said pointing high into the hills.

"No," Ranger Foss said. "They wouldn't have."

"Why not?" Lacey replied. "They've hiked every trail in this park hundreds of times."

"They couldn't know," Morris said.

"I hope you're right."

With Savannah in the lead, the girls walked quickly towards the trailhead. As they walked past the main trial, and headed towards the large beach and swimming area, Jennifer rushed up to Savannah and stopped her.

"Savannah," Jennifer said getting in front of her, "the trailhead is that way. We need to get on that trail right away."

"Just trust me," she said. "We're going to the beach first. Greg has a thing for that one lifeguard girl that works here. Let's see if she working this morning and if she saw them at all."

"Is the beach even open yet?" Heidi asked, looking at her watch.

"The lifeguards will be there," Savannah said. "Making sure the beach is clear and doing other maintenance things. She always works mornings—the hobbit with the massive rack. What's her name again?"

"Brandi," Jennifer said. "Okay then, we need to be quick though." Savannah nodded and started off again; the others followed.

The beach was empty when they got there. A moment later, they saw Brandi pushing a cart of cleaning supplies from the bathrooms. Brandi was only five feet tall, with thick brown hair that went to her waist. Brandi, wearing only a red lifeguard bathing suit, was in the process of her morning routine. The girls rushed up to her.

"Hey Brandi!" Savannah shouted as they got near her.

"Hey," Brandi said as she noticed them and waved. "What brings you out here on a Tuesday? Shouldn't you be in college, learning something so you don't end up like me? Twenty-eight and working an entry level job?"

"Cute," Savannah said, towering over the shorter girl. "Lower your standards and marry some rich bozo, someone like Greg. Speaking of Greg, you didn't happen to see him this weekend have you?"

"Can't say that I have," Brandi said. "I'm sure that if he was here he would have sought me out. I've been here every morning. He always finds me."

"Hard enough to do," Savannah said. "You can hide so easily."

"Big bird makes a short joke," Brandi said. "They're talking it might rain this evening. Want to give me a warning before I get wet?"

"Enough," Heidi said, bored. "You two flirting with each other is getting us nowhere. I need to be back tomorrow. We need to find them."

"Lost your boys?" Brandi asked. "Haven't seen them. If I do, I'll tell them you're looking for them."

"Thanks," Jennifer said as she started walking away. The group followed Jennifer, but Savannah paused, about to say something more but deciding against it. She quickly caught up with the others.

"Why are you always so hard on her?" Jennifer asked.

"She asks for it," Savannah said. "When I started running here there were some guys that always hung out on the beach. I was trying to put something together, get them to notice me, but she ruined that. You have no idea how hard it is for a tall, muscular girl to find a decent guy. The only ones who ever approach me are freaks."

Jennifer was about to respond when a group of four guys met them on the trail. The guys looked college aged, wearing swimming trunks and baseball caps.

"Hello ladies," the front man grinned flirtatiously. "How's the beach this morning?"

"Real good," Savannah said.

"How's 'bout you lovely ladies come back to the beach with us?" he asked. "You could watch us play a little Frisbee."

"Watch you play?" Savannah scoffed. "I'd rather watch paint dry."

"Feisty," the man said, "I like that. You all look pretty fit; how 'bout an Ultimate Frisbee match? Four-on-four and we'll let you sub your extra in anytime you want."

"When I play sports," Savannah said. "I only play when there's a real challenge. You'd be too easy. We've got a schedule to keep. Sorry, boys." With that, Savannah pushed her way past the group and the others followed her. The man shrugged his shoulders and started leading his friends back towards the beach. Savannah and the girls continued to the trailhead.

As they were walking, a tall, lanky man approached them. The man was wearing an outfit that looked to be from the 1800's, jeans, long-sleeved shirt, vest, with a Stetson hat and cowboy boots.

"Hello," the man said.

"Hello," Savannah said, wary of him. "Beautiful day, sir."

"Don't go into the woods today," the man said. The girls stopped and looked at him. The man appeared to be very serious, but also in a lot of pain.

"Why not?" Leah took a drink from her flask. "Are the teddy bears having a picnic?"

"I wouldn't make jokes at a time like this, Leah," the man said. The women took a step back, scared.

"How the hell did you know my name?" Leah asked. "Who are you?" The women studied his serious face. He stood powerfully and looked to be in his late thirties. Savannah stepped between the man and the other women.

"Look, cowboy," Savannah said. "I don't know who you are, but leave us alone."

"Please Savannah," the man said. "You won't find what you're looking for. Just go home. Jennifer, I beg you, go home."

"Come on," Savannah said. "Keep moving. Don't you dare follow us."

Savannah ushered her friends along, wanting to put some distance between them and the cowboy. Jennifer looked back at him, wondering if she should try to find out more, but Savannah grabbed her arm and moved her along.

"How did he know our names?" Leah asked breaking the silence.

"Most likely," Savannah said, "he saw us arrive and saw the names written on the parking slip on the cars. Old bastard is probably some pervert that saw a group of girls and thought that he could get some action. Thought we'd be up for an orgy or something."

"I don't know," Jennifer said. "There was something about him. Something I can't put my finger on."

"You could say that about any stranger that walked up to you and gave you a random warning," Savannah said. "We need to move."

The women rushed along, making it to the trailhead before taking the foothill trail that led along the river. They jogged down the trail, along its gentle rolling hills, not wasting any time on the scenery. They were on a mission to get to their friends as quickly as they possibly could. As they came around a corner, Savannah motioned them to stop. She studied the north side of the trail; it didn't take long before she saw the start of the hidden trail.

Chapter 4

The group gazed at where Savannah was standing. It was barely visible, but within the trees and grass were the remnants of a trail. As Savannah pulled out her GPS device, Leah pulled out a flask and took a drink. Savannah played with her GPS for a moment before pulling out a map and compass. She looked toward the sky and took some notes on the map before putting everything away.

"What are you doing?" Heidi asked. "What's all that for?"

"There are questions that haven't been answered, let alone asked," Savannah said looking closer at the trail. "What if they guys got up into the foothills, got turned around, and are lost? I marked this point on my GPS so we will have a guide to get back, just in case."

"Smart thinking," Jennifer said.

"Lost?" Roxy asked. "What if we get lost? We could die up there."

"But we won't," Savannah said.

"But what if…" Roxy started.

"Roxy," Savannah said walking up to her, "I can guide us through any forest, and I will make sure we all survive."

"How can you be so sure?" Roxy asked.

"I've hunted with my family for years," Savannah said. "I've taken down a lot of different animals—mainly with a bow, but I've used guns too. I've trekked over twenty miles to get to a base camp. I've tracked elk for miles, read the trees, and anything else you can think of. My family is military; they taught me everything I know. Hunting, tracking, fighting, and survival are in my blood. I can get us through this, but I need something from you."

"What?" Roxy asked meekly.

"Believe in me," Savannah said. "If you trust me, nothing will stop us and we'll be back at school in no time, okay?"

"Okay," Roxy said.

"Now, that being said," Savannah said looked back at the trail, "I need to ask a question. Do any of you want to back out now? You can go back, sit this one out, and no one will think any less of you for it." No one said anything. They all had their eyes locked on Savannah, trying to figure out what she was going to do next.

"No?" Savannah asked. "Good. If this trip gets hard, or things get difficult, I want no belly aching, pissing, bitching, or moaning. I asked if you wanted to do this and you are all coming along willingly."

"I have one question?" Jennifer said. "We're going to get my fiancée, who the hell made you leader?"

"I did," Savannah said, getting right in Jennifer's face. Savannah took a powerful, firm posture and stood tall and dominant, looming over Jennifer. "I know beyond a shadow of a doubt that I'm the best person to lead this group, so I'm going to lead it. You've always followed me on these trips, whenever we've gone on an adventure. Hell, even the guys followed my lead. They knew that I was the best choice, and that if any of them challenged me I could kick their ass.

"Jennifer, the further we go in the woods, the longer we go without seeing the guys, the more emotionally drained you're going to become. Trust me. We need someone with a clear head and a sharp mind to lead this expedition. You know that I'm the most level headed out of us. Do you disagree with any of that?"

"No," Jennifer said quickly. "I just want Mike back."

"I want him back too," Savannah said. "I can't wait to see you as a bride. Now everyone take out your phones." They all complied. "I told you to download a GPS app on your phone. Open it up and mark this spot as our starting location."

"Why?" Heidi asked. "You have already done that. Why do we need to as well?"

"Because every time we stop, we're going to mark our location," Savannah said. "If we get separated and lost we go back to the last rally point. Never set a point unless we all do."

"You really do know a lot about this," Leah said.

"Dad trained me to be a military leader," Savannah said. "Another time I disappointed him; I took accounting in college and didn't sign up to be all I could be. Saddle up, ladies, follow me and stay silent."

Savannah slung her pack over her shoulder and started down the trail. The trail was hard to spot, and some of the others didn't even know if they were on it at all, but Savannah could see the path the guys had followed. The first few hundred feet were difficult, through heavy underbrush, trees, and long grass, but as they lost sight of the main trail, a better trail emerged.

Savannah stopped as they entered onto the path. She surveyed the area and took a closer look at the trail. They were in a heavily wooded area, mainly maple trees with a few dogwoods, cottonwoods, and oak interspersed. The floor was a grassy moss mixture with no small undergrowth. The trail was a small clearing through the trees, barely visible, but cleared by heavy animal use. The girls couldn't see far into the trees; the growth was too thick.

Satisfied everything was safe, Savannah motioned and the girls started walking again. Savannah led them at a quick pace, twisting and turning on the trail, going up and down the rolling hills, all the while keeping a sharp eye out for any signs of their friends.

As they were walking, almost jogging, not taking any time to enjoy the beauty of the forest around them, Savannah came to a sudden stop. She motioned for the others to get down. The girls all crouched down behind Savannah as she stared intently into the trees, looking for something. Savannah kept her hand up, indicating that she wanted them to be completely silent. At first, the girls couldn't figure out what was going on, but then a twig snapped.

Everyone froze, scared. Heidi was almost ready to bolt. Leah took a pull from her flask as Roxy held back tears. Jennifer hoped it was Mike. Savannah pointed to a spot in the trees and smiled. The girls looked, but there was nothing at first. Then a beautiful, monstrous moose broke through the tree line and lumbered past the girls. All the girls breathed a sigh of relief. Savannah mimed shooting an arrow at the majestic creature.

"If I could bag that, I bet I would beat my brother's record," Savannah said. "His head would make a fine trophy on the wall, but I bet his meat would be old and tough."

"Barbaric," Roxy said.

"Not really," Savannah replied standing up. "Even a hundred years ago we were reliant on hunted food."

"In this day and age," Roxy said, "you hunters are disgusting. Go to the store."

"I would love a reality show," Savannah said, "that puts whiny, tree-hugging snots like you in the forest and watches you fend for yourselves. Without a wally-world on every corner, you'd starve to death in a week. I could live my life here and never be hungry, never want."

"Some people have evolved," Roxy sneered, "while others still live like cavemen."

"Remember when I said no whining?" Savannah asked as she started walking. "I'm certain we agreed to no whining."

"Enough," Jennifer said. "Keep moving."

Savannah nodded and picked up the pace of the group. She was excited by the fact that she could still see shoeprints in the forest floor. She wasn't sure if it was their guys, but she couldn't imagine that other people had recently been on this trail, plus she was able to see four distinct shoe patterns. Savannah knew that they were on the right path.

The women jogged quietly although the temperatures were starting to break past ninety and the sun wasn't fully in the sky. Everyone was sweating and Savannah knew that very soon they'd need a break, a chance to rest, rehydrate, and eat something. Savannah was hoping to find more concrete evidence of the guys when they broke out of the forest and into a clearing.

The sight they saw caused them all to stop in their tracks. There was a grassy meadow in the woods, about a twenty-acre patch with a river running through it, coming down from the tops of the mountains. The meadow was bright and vibrant, with green grass, yellow and white clover, and blue flowers. The smell of the flowers in bloom was so aromatic that it was almost overpowering. The meadow could have been featured in any nature show or on any postcard, but it wasn't the natural beauty that caused the girls to stop. It was the two tents by the river, Mike and Todd's tents.

Jennifer was about to rush into the clearing when Savannah grabbed her by the arm and pulled her back. Savannah pushed Jennifer behind her before looking out over the clearing. She dug in her pack and pulled out a black Glock 9mm handgun, loaded and ready to go. The other women stepped back, freaked out.

"What in the hell are you doing with that?" Jennifer asked.

"Quiet," Savannah said. Savannah looked around before slowly walking into the clearing, motioning for them to stay back. Savannah got almost all the way to the tents before she waved to the others closer. Jennifer sprinted forward and almost ripped the zipper door off Mike's tent.

As Jennifer went through Mike's tent, Savannah and Heidi examined Todd's. There was clothing spread around the floor mixed in with other supplies. It was a mess.

"Looks about like Todd and Greg's rooms," Savannah said. "That's their bags." Heidi didn't look to where Savannah was pointing. She was looking over a pile of clothing. Something had caught her eye, an article of clothing that she needed to do a double take on. Heidi bent down and picked up two things before turning to Savannah.

"I knew Todd and Greg were strange," Heidi said holding a yellow bikini top in one hand, a white sports bra in the other. "But I didn't think they were this freaky." She tossed the bra to Savannah who looked at the tag.

"Size small," Savannah said. "Don't think those boys could fit into this even if they wanted to."

"This is also a small," Heidi said. "Even I couldn't fit into it."

"Looks like the size a teenage girl would wear," Savannah said.

"Fourteen or fifteen-year-old," Heidi said.

"Any other goods?" Savannah asked pushing some clothes piles around. "Any bottoms? Condoms? Things that shouldn't be here?"

"Doesn't look like it," Heidi said pushing some clothing around with her foot. "Nothing to indicate that anything happened here."

"Let's see if the others found anything," Savannah said tossing the bra down. Savannah exited the tent while Heidi took the bikini and the bra and placed them underneath a pile of clothing so that they wouldn't be seen if someone entered the tent and took a quick look around. Heidi gave a final glance around the tent before she exited to the group.

"Mike!" Jennifer shouted. "Mike! Where are you?"

"Keep your voice down," Savannah said walking up to Jennifer. "We don't want to attract any animals."

Jennifer looked at Savannah. She couldn't figure out how Savannah could be so calm while Jennifer's future was up in the air. She knew that the guys meant something to Savannah, even if she always acted too tough to care. Jennifer looked over the group. Savannah was scanning the area with her gun drawn. Heidi exited the tent looking confused. Roxy tried to stay close to Savannah, but so close as to make it obvious. Leah sat by the river having a drink.

"What do you think we should do?" Jennifer asked Savannah. "You're in charge. What's the right move here?"

"Set up camp," Savannah said. "We base here. It's far enough in the foothills that we can cover a bigger area. We set camp, eat, and then move out. I can tell that there are four trails that extend from this area, not including the one we walked in on. I will have to check each one of them out to see where the guys went."

"Then we split up?" Heidi asked. "We could search two trails at the same time and cover more ground."

"I go with Savannah," Roxy said quickly.

"We do not," Savannah said.

"Why not?" Jennifer asked. "We could cover more ground. We could find them quicker."

"Listen to me, Jennifer," Savannah said. "Trust me, we do not want to split up. That would be a very bad idea."

"Why?" Jennifer asked.

"Yeah," Heidi chimed in. "Why would it be bad?"

"Because," Savannah said, taking a deep breath. "We don't know what happened to them. We have to assume that there is a threat in these woods. If there is a threat, you don't want to divide your forces. That's what an aggressive enemy wants, ever hear of divide and conquer?"

"You know so much about this military stuff," Heidi said. "Yet you want to be an accountant and not a soldier?"

"Don't ever talk to me like that again, Heidi," Savannah said with a growl. "We need to keep our troop strong."

"You think that there's a threat out here?" Roxy asked. "Like bears or mountain men?"

"I don't know, Roxy," Savannah said. "But I'm doing what will keep us the strongest. On that note, we need to eat. Heidi, you're the best with the tents, set them up. We stay here. If the guys come back they need to find us."

"What if they were attacked here?" Heidi said. "Huh? Then we're sitting ducks, you ever think of that?"

"Yes, I did," Savannah said holding up the gun. "That's why when we sleep tonight, we will set up watch."

"You really know a lot about this stuff," Roxy said. "How did you learn it all?"

"I have six older brothers," Savannah said. "All tough guys, military like my dad. I've read their books, gone through survival training, things like that. I was raised like a soldier. Mom and dad didn't want any girls so when they had one, they just pretended I was a boy. A big strong man they could be proud of, not some wimpy little girl that had to be protected."

"You must have gotten beaten up a lot growing up then," Heidi said.

"Until I was big enough to defend myself," Savannah said. "While you played Barbie, I had G.I. Joe. You played Candyland? I learned military strategy with Risk, Stratego, and Axis and Allies. Just follow my lead and listen to what I say. I'll get us through this."

"We trust you Savannah," Heidi said. "What's our move?"

"Get the camp setup and eat," Savannah said. "Then we move out."

Chapter 5

The forest was a symphony of animal sounds as they trekked along on the barely-there trail that followed the river to the north and higher into the foothills. The women didn't speak as they walked quickly. Jennifer was getting more upset as every hour went by without a sign of their guys. Mike was the only thing on her mind; she couldn't imagine not finding him.

As the trail moved higher into the hills, the air seemed to get warmer. All the girls were sweating heavily but Savannah, who was conditioned by years of high school and college sports, didn't seem to mind. The others, who weren't as strong as she was, were having trouble keeping up the pace Savannah set. There were many times when one of the girls wanted to stop and take a break, but Savannah never gave them the chance to even express their concern.

As they rounded a bend in the river, they stopped in their tracks. Savannah pulled the gun from its holster clipped to her tight shorts. The girls could see the ruins of old equipment in a clearing along the river. The area wasn't big, but there were a lot of old items strewn about: large, bug looking pieces of rusted iron with cables and chains hanging everywhere. A tall pole stuck out of the ground and there were remains of a pier in the river. Savannah jumped up onto a stump to get a better look around.

"What is this place?" Roxy asked in a hushed voice.

"An abandoned logging site," Savannah said. "That tall pole with the cables is a spar. They would use that to bring the logs to the river with a system of cables and pulleys. One end attached to the log, the other to a pack animal. I don't think a tractor could run on this terrain."

"How the hell did they get all this stuff out here?" Heidi asked. "I mean, is there a bigger trail somewhere?"

"We have no idea how big the hidden trail use to be," Savannah said. "It could have very easily been big enough to bring all this equipment here. This place may have been intended to be a logging site. The ranger's station and surrounding buildings do look like they could have been a logging camp at one point in time."

"What does this mean?" Jennifer asked. "Where are the guys?"

"This is why the trail was abandoned," Savannah said. "I would bet on it. They didn't want salvagers coming through here. The equipment was abandoned when the camp failed."

"This place is haunted," Roxy said. "I bet that's why they abandoned it. We need to get out of here before we upset the spirits."

"Shut up," Savannah said. "Most likely, this place was annexed into a state forest and the logging had to stop. The terrain would make it difficult to log here, so I bet they moved somewhere more cost effective. Once the loggers were gone and the park formed, it wasn't anything to worry about until people started wanting the metal. The park didn't want the junk being hauled through the forest—think of the damage that could cause, so they hid the trails and never mentioned them again."

"That makes sense," Roxy said. "So there's no angry, logger ghosts floating about?"

"None," Savannah said. "You don't need to worry about it."

"At least that makes sense," Jennifer said as she paced. "But that still doesn't get us one bit closer to finding the guys. We need to pick up the search. We need to split up."

"Why don't you fire a shot in the air," Roxy said. "The guys would hear the gun and come running."

"There are so many things wrong with that idea, Roxy," Savannah said. "I need to conserve the rounds, never know when we're going to get into a firefight. Jennifer, we cannot split up. We need to investigate this area and the surrounding area. I bet the guys were looking for cool places to take us when we came here."

"That makes sense," Jennifer said.

"Everybody stick close," Savannah said. "Keep your eyes on the ground. There could be lots of old metal, broken machine parts, or damaged trees around here. I don't want to have to carry you out because you twisted your ankle not paying attention to where you were walking."

They all nodded and followed Savannah through the logging area. She inspected all the equipment, the rotted out log piles, the docks on the river, and the surrounding area. They looked over the area over for almost an hour before they walked to a high swell of land on the west side of the logging site.

"Anybody see anything that would indicate the guys were here?" Jennifer asked.

"Nothing," Leah said taking a drink from her flask.

"I didn't see anything either," Heidi said.

"I know that the guys started on the trail we left the camp from," Savannah said. "There weren't tracks on any of the other trails."

"Could they have gone on a different path?" Jennifer asked. "Could there have been a side trail that we missed? There could have been, right?"

"I was tracking their tracks," Savannah said. "I didn't see tracks that looked like theirs. There was a couple, but they're not as prominent as the prints we followed."

"Great," Jennifer said throwing her arms up. "Super hunter doesn't know what tracks to follow. Why are we even listening to you? We should split up and search more ground."

"Stop," Savannah said. "Look over there."

Savannah pointed north, upriver. At first, they couldn't see anything, but they realized that the trees were moving. Everywhere else was still, no breeze, but a pair of trees moved like there was a strong breeze. As the trees danced, Jennifer started to walk forward, but Savannah stopped her.

"Let me go," Jennifer said. "It could be them."

"It's not," Savannah said. "I don't know what it is. But if we don't understand it, we don't go rushing into it. It could be a trap."

"Trap?" Roxy said swallowing in a throat suddenly dry. "Who would want to trap us?"

"She's just trying to scare us," Jennifer said trying to walk towards the trees again.

"No, I'm not," Savannah said stopping Jennifer again.

"Let me go!" Jennifer shouted, trying to push her off. "I have to find him!"

"Getting yourself killed won't help him," Savannah said. Jennifer tried to get Savannah to let her go, but Savannah was far too powerful. They struggled for a moment before Jennifer tried to punch Savannah. Savannah easily blocked the shot and quickly took Jennifer to the ground, holding her down, not giving her a chance to get up. Jennifer struggled, but soon realized that Savannah wasn't joking around.

"Enough," Savannah said as the others looked on not knowing what to do. "We went through this when we started. I am running this rescue mission. You have to understand, Jennifer. I want to save them. That's all I'm concerned with right now. You need to realize that something happened to them. If they weren't in trouble, they would have contacted us. They're lost, hurt, or captured. If they were okay, we wouldn't be here. I have to be in command here. You're too emotional right now. Roxy's too scared. Heidi's just along for the ride. Leah's almost drunk. Please follow my lead. I promise you that I will do everything in my power to get us and the guys out of here safely and quickly, but I need your help. You need to keep your head for me. Can you keep it together for me, Jennifer?"

"Let me up," Jennifer said struggling.

"Can you keep it together for me? Can you keep it together for Mike?"

Jennifer struggled under Savannah for a moment, but she knew there was no way she would be able to break free. Jennifer had a flash though; with as domineering as Savannah was being, she could convince the others to follow her. When they were back at the camp, Jennifer knew that she could get the others to follow her. Jennifer stopped struggling and looked Savannah in the eyes.

"Sorry, Savannah," Jennifer said. "I'm so worried about Mike. I can't even describe it. All I want is to get him back. Thank you so much for leading us. Please let me up."

Savannah paused for a moment before letting Jennifer back up. As she got up Savannah looked back towards the trees that had been moving, and now they were as still as the rest of the forest. Savannah, with her gun drawn, walked slowly over to the trees, and looked around. There were no tracks, prints, or anything to indicate that anyone had been there. Savannah jogged back to her friends.

"There's nothing here," Savannah said. "We need to keep moving."

"We going deeper into the hills?" Jennifer asked.

"No," Savannah said. "These trails loop around. We are going to take a different way back to the camp, see if we can find any traces of them on a different trail."

"You sure the trails loop together?" Heidi asked.

"Positive," Savannah said. "We need to keep moving though, I don't want to be away from the campsite at night."

"Lead the way, Savannah," Jennifer said.

Savannah started to walk at her near-jogging pace. The group followed her onto a different trail than the one they had come on. They struggled to keep up with Savannah as she rushed along the trail. This trail was slightly wider than the one they had been on before, but rougher, strewn with rocks and potholes where there wasn't bare ground. Savannah looked for tracks or any indication that the guys had been here, but she couldn't find anything.

As they neared the campsite, the sun was dipping towards the horizon. Savannah stopped the group. She motioned them to stay back, away from where she was standing. Savannah dropped onto her knees and looked very closely at the ground. Savannah was positive that she could see some form of tracks, shoe prints, but she couldn't be sure they were from the guys. There were two different sets of prints along with some tracks that looked older, but Savannah couldn't be sure.

The others watched and wondered at what Savannah was doing. Jennifer contemplated how she was going to get the others to turn against Savannah and follow her. Leah was hoping she'd have enough vodka to make it back to her bottle at the campsite. Roxy was scared that something would find them in the woods. Heidi was hoping that they would find the guys soon so they could get back to campus.

"What is it, Savannah?" Heidi asked. "Is there something there?"

"Tracks," Savannah said standing up. "Can't positively identify if the guys left them or not. There's only two prints here for sure, and they look older than what we need."

"Do we follow them?" Jennifer asked.

"Not now," Savannah said. "They are not good enough to consider right now. We'll try some other trails tomorrow morning, there were some better tracks near the camp that I want to follow. We need to keep moving though."

Savannah led the girls along down the trail. It didn't take them much time to reach the campsite. When the girls broke through the trees and saw the site the girls stopped dead in their tracks, their jaws hanging on the ground, stunned at what they saw; the girl's tents were just as they'd left them, the guy's tents had been taken down and were gone without a trace.

"What the hell is going on?" Jennifer asked angrily.

"Damned if I know," Savannah said. "This pisses me off."

"Why didn't they wait for us?" Roxy asked.

"Maybe they couldn't," Savannah said.

"What?" Heidi asked. "Why wouldn't they?"

"Injury," Savannah said. "But they should have either left one person here or left us a note of some kind to let us know what's going on. The rest of you stay here, Heidi, come with me. We need to search the tents and the area."

Chapter 6

As the night owls hooted eerily and the stars twinkled in the sky, Leah paced the perimeter of the campsite, handgun in one hand, flask in the other. Leah had never been afraid of the dark, but tonight there was something on her mind, something that she couldn't seem to shake. She was concerned for the guys, and hoped they would find them soon, but there was something else. She felt eyes watching her, but not too closely.

Every new animal sound, every wolf howl, fox call, and moose grunt would cause Leah to jump and point the pistol in a new direction. She was on edge and was using alcohol to try and take the edge off. Leah realized that she was buzzed, near drunk, but she felt better that way. She'd been in that state for almost the entire semester.

When they'd returned to the camp, and saw that the other tents were gone, Savannah and Heidi had searched the area, but didn't find any notes or anything disturbed in their tents. There was no trace of who had taken the tents down or where they had gone. Savannah had seemed to notice several things, but wouldn't tell anyone what she was discovering or why it was important. Leah took another drink from her flask as she heard a tent zipper open.

Leah looked back to the camp and saw Savannah exiting one of the tents. Leah breathed a sigh of relief. She had been given the first watch and Savannah had the second. Leah whistled to her friend so Savannah could tell where she was. Leah looked over her friend as she was bathed in the silver moonlight. Savannah was a powerful woman who carried herself to reflect that.

Savannah was wearing red and gray, baggy soccer shorts with her college number, 04, sewn onto the leg, with a black, athletic bikini top. Leah could see how muscular Savannah was, how impressively powerful her body was. Leah was glad that she never had to face Savannah in any sports. Savannah motioned for the gun and Leah handed it to her.

"Anything happen?" Savannah asked.

"Nothing notable," Leah said. "The animals are out tonight. Listen to them." Savannah listened to the songs being sung and smiled.

"If the animals are singing," Savannah said, "then all is right with the forest. Tomorrow will be a good day."

"I'm going to bed then," Leah said.

"Hang on," Savannah said motioning to a log to sit down on. "I need to talk to you." Savannah and Leah sat down on a log. Savannah was silent for a moment as Leah took another pull from her flask before offering it to Savannah, who waved it off.

"What is it?" Leah asked.

"Why are you drinking so much?" Savannah asked.

"What?"

"You've been drinking heavily," Savannah said. "Don't deny it. This past semester, you always have a flask with you. There's got to be a reason, what is it?"

"There's nothing wrong," Leah said.

"Don't do that to me, Leah," Savannah said turning towards her friend. "Don't shut me out. You were there for me. Let me be there for you."

"That was different," Leah said taking another drink. "You just got injured, big deal."

"Big deal?" Savannah almost yelled. "Look Leah, all my life I was ignored by my parents and beaten up and bullied by my brothers. The only way I could get any attention at all was in sports. They wanted a volleyball player, but my love was soccer. I became the soccer star in my high school. My brothers had all been captains and champions in football and wrestling. I was a soccer and track star."

"You did well in gymnastics too," Leah said.

"Not really," Savannah said. "I never made it past sections and any time the team went to state I always dragged us down. Gymnastics wasn't my favorite thing."

"Why did you do it then?" Leah asked.

"Good way to stay in shape over the winter," Savannah said. "It was a good training sport, but most importantly, when I was in gymnastics, in my bright pink leotard covered in red hearts, with pink ribbons in my hair, it drove my parent's nuts. They made it known to me they only wanted boys, so I used gymnastics to rub it in a little."

"But I've seen your soccer video," Leah said. "In double overtime, a score of 0-0, you get a kick that wins the high school state championship. They must have loved that."

"That was the greatest moment of my life," Savannah said. "That was the only time in my life that my parents said they were proud of me. I was so happy."

"You had a good college career too," Leah said.

"The first three years," Savannah said. "But then I blew out my knee. All I wanted was to play professional soccer. That's what I was working for. I know I was good enough. I know I could have been the best. I'm still better than most people, but with the way they rebuilt my knee there's no way that I can perform at the levels that I was at before." Savannah wiped a tear from her eye. "All I wanted was to be a sports star, and I was, but now I'm nothing."

"Come on, Savannah," Leah said, "you have a great job lined up."

"I'm gonna be an accountant," Savannah said.

"Yeah," Leah said, "you're going to be paid triple what I'm getting, plus you get benefits and you work in a nice office."

"You get to work in the forest," Savannah said. "You can wear outdoor clothing, I have to wear skirts and blouses...yuck."

"And I have to keep a part-time job so I can make ends meet," Leah said. "There's nothing wrong with being an accountant. It's an honest living and you make good money."

"Both my parents are military," Savannah said. "As were all six of my brothers. Four are still serving, two died overseas. Think about that Leah, my parents wanted military men and I'm an accountant girl. You know they didn't even invite me to Christmas last year? Once they found out my sports career was over they forgot about me."

Savannah was on the verge of crying. Leah offered her the flask again, but Savannah passed. Leah leaned in and hugged her friend. She wasn't sure what she should do, but she'd never seen Savannah without her tough façade before. Leah squeezed her tight.

"I love you, Savannah," Leah said. "We all do. Your team loves you and I'm sure that all the people at your work are going to love you. One day, you'll find a nice man who'll love you and you two will be really happy together."

"Yeah right," Savannah said. "Jesus Christ, I was trying to cheer you up and figure out what's wrong and here I am spilling my guts, crying on your shoulder."

"It seemed like you needed to talk more than I did," Leah said. "I've never seen you like this. You always act so tough. I mean, you are tough, but everyone needs to let it out every once in a while."

"Thanks," Savannah said composing herself. "Now your drinking, what's the story?"

"Damned if I know," Leah said.

"Come on," Savannah said. "Let me in. I opened up. How long have we been friends?"

"A long time," Leah said sighing heavily. "Okay. When I was in eighth grade there were some injuries on the varsity basketball team. I was the superstar of the junior varsity team so I got called up to the varsity team. The first varsity game I played was a rivalry game against a big team. I was big for an eighth grader, but tiny compared to these girls. The decision to dress me varsity was made that day so I didn't even get a varsity practice. I was so excited, but when I saw the other team warming up I knew I was in trouble. The game was tight, back and forth, and the stands were packed, more people than I'd ever played in front of before. After eight minutes of playtime, the score 18-18, the coach put me in. I was so nervous. The girl I was supposed to cover was over a foot taller than I was. I was just going in for a moment so the coach could give some strategy to who I was subbing for. The ball goes into play, I rush down the court, and they pass me the ball. I froze, literally froze, standing there with the ball. Every person in the stands was looking at me and my mind went blank. I couldn't even remember what I was supposed to do. People were yelling, but I couldn't hear any of them. I knew I needed to do something so I started to dribble the ball and move back, the only problem, the giants of the other team were moving in, I stepped on one of their foots, got myself tripped up, and ended up looking at the lights with a girl sixty pounds heavier than I was on top of me."

"Oh my God," Savannah laughed. "That's hilarious."

"Not really," Leah said.

"Why haven't you ever told me this story before?" Savannah asked. "I thought I knew all you good basketball stories?"

"It's embarrassing," Leah said. "At first, I wanted to laugh because someone was screaming, then I realized it was me and I realized how much my leg hurt. The big girl quickly stood up but she fell back on top of me, also screaming. She'd twisted her knee and sprained her ankle. I'd broken my ankle. I'd been in less than fifteen seconds. I had to be carried out of the gym, with all those people watching me. It was horrible."

"How'd the game turn out?" Savannah asked.

"That girl was a senior captain," Leah said. "The girls quickly said they were dedicating this game to her. They rallied and won, 67-55. The point is, I feel like that again, when they gave me the ball. I feel like there are all these eyes on me, waiting for me to act, but my mind is blank and I'm frozen. Something I haven't told any of you, this job I have lined up is only for a year, a temporary gig. My parents are telling me I should find something full-time, but I have no idea what I want. I really want to stay in college. I'm not ready for the real world."

"None of us are," Savannah said. "It's nice where we are now. College is familiar. We can party it up and have fun without responsibility."

"I don't want to leave," Leah said. "I don't want to leave us and our group."

"You know," Savannah said, "I bet you said the same thing when you graduated high school. It's always like that. You find something comfortable and you don't want to leave it."

"It's something that I hate," Leah said. "Everything parents and schools do now is to make us feel comfortable. But now we're getting kicked out and we're not ready for it. They think that they are doing something good for us, but they really aren't."

"I know how you feel," Savannah said. "Things are rough, but they will get better."

"What made you pick accounting?" Leah asked. "I mean, if you were going to be a sports star, why work so hard for an accounting degree?"

"I was always good at math," Savannah said. "And I've heard about college stars who put everything into their sport who don't make it. Then, they have nothing to fall back on. I knew I couldn't count on my parents, so I picked something I can make a decent living at."

"You were always smart," Leah said. "And level headed." Savannah looked at her friend. It'd been a long time since they'd both been this open with each other and Savannah really enjoyed it. As she was leaning in to hug her friend, the girls heard a massive twig snap. It sounded like there were footsteps outside of the campsite. Savannah motioned for Leah to get down. Both women crouched down behind the log they'd been sitting on.

As the sounds of the forest went silent, the footsteps got louder and louder. Savannah tried to see what was making the sounds, keeping her gun at the ready. As they looked, Leah pointed to where she thought she saw a shadow moving in the darkness. Savannah caught a glimpse of it.

"What is it?" Leah whispered.

"Quiet," Savannah said. They kept watch, trying to see, but there was nothing in the trees. It was in a moment, sheer terror as both girls felt a cold breeze rush over their bodies, four figures stepped out of the woods and into the clearing. The figures were human-like, big, and it looked like they were searching for something. Savannah and Leah held their breath as the figures looked around the campsite. They stayed on the one side of the campsite, near where they had entered.

It was only a minute, but felt like a lifetime, before the figures started to move back into the woods. As the last one stood in the clearing, it turned and looked at Leah and Savannah behind the log. Its eyes were glowing blue, but they couldn't see any kind of face. It looked at them for a heartbeat before disappearing into the woods. The girls were frozen as the noise of the forest started up again.

"What the hell was that?" Leah asked.

"I have no idea," Savannah said. "They were bigger than any of our guys. I don't know what that could have been."

"Mountain men?" Leah asked.

"I don't know," Savannah said.

"Should we follow them?" Leah asked.

"No," Savannah said. "We need to keep a close watch tonight and we'll track them in the morning. You should head to bed though, rest up for the morning."

"Okay," Leah said. "Will you be okay out here by yourself?"

"Yeah," Savannah said. "Thanks. I should be fine. Don't tell the others about this. I don't think they need to know."

"Why not?" Leah asked.

"Roxy's too scared the way it is," Savannah said, "and every minute we don't find Mike, Jennifer gets more upset. I'm afraid that she might do something drastic."

"Okay," Leah said. "Thanks for talking to me tonight. It helped just to talk about it."

"Any time," Savannah said hugging her friend.

"Goodnight," Leah said.

"Night," Savannah said as Leah walked to the tent.

Savannah checked the clip of her gun. She had fifteen rounds in the clip and one in the chamber. Savannah felt confident that she could keep the group safe, but she was more worried about the others keeping their heads. She was impressed by how well Leah handled seeing the shadows. Savannah knew that the morning would come all too soon and tomorrow would be a long day.

Chapter 7

Lacey and Brandi were already busy repainting the lettering on signs that were positioned around the beach when the sun peaked over the horizon. It was a hot a sticky morning that held the promise of being a sweltering day. As the women put the finishing touches on the signs, Morris drove up on an ATV followed by two police officers, each on their own ATV. The girls put down their brushes as Morris and the cops approached.

"What's up, Morris?" Lacey asked. "What's with the police?"

"This is Officers Thompson and Smith," Morris said. "They are here to get some information about the missing guys."

"Those boys haven't been seen yet?" Brandi asked.

"No sightings reported," Morris said.

"When was the last time anyone saw them?" Officer Smith asked.

"When they arrived," Lacey said. "They didn't talk to anyone, they just went right out onto the trails."

"And there was no trace of them when you were searching for the missing teenage girls?" Officer Thompson asked.

"None," Morris said. "I even went past where they said they would be camping at. I had a thought that the girls may have crossed their paths and they went with them to the guy's campsite, but the guys had never been to where they said they were camping."

"And their car is parked within the State Forest grounds?"

"In the main parking lot," Lacey said. "Right next to the girl's car."

"Girl's car?" Officer Thompson asked.

"The guys were part of a group of friends," Lacey said. "There are four guys and five girls. They hiked, swam, and camped here pretty frequently. They were always together. Yesterday morning, the girls arrived and went into the woods right away. They were determined to find their guys."

"Why did the girls go in?" Officer Smith asked. "Why not just wait for us?"

"One of the girls," Lacey said. "Implied that the guys may be smoking some dope. They didn't want the police to find them and get them in trouble. They graduate in a couple weeks."

"Has anyone seen them since?" Officer Thompson asked.

"They came to me right away," Brandi said. "One of the guys had a thing for me so they thought I might know where they were at. I didn't. They took off and bumped into a group of guys that have been here for a few days. The guys offered to play some Frisbee with them, but they said they had a schedule to keep and took off into the woods."

"That's the last anyone's seen of them too," Morris said. "I gave them a walkie-talkie to keep in contact with the main office, but when I tried to contact them this morning, I didn't get any response."

"Do you have any idea where they could have gone?" Officer Smith asked.

"No," Morris answered quickly. "They were last seen entering the main trailhead. They gave us no indication as to which trails they were going to be walking."

"Interesting," Officer Smith said. "Seems this park has a history of people going missing. More than any other park in the state. Forty missing hikers in the past fifteen years."

"There's some dangerous waters," Lacey said. "The rivers look good for swimming, maybe they think they can dive from a tree into the river, but the water is shallow and fast. We know it's happened. If they do that on the rivers to the west of the park, the water moves too quickly to find the bodies."

"We are going to do some searching," Officer Thompson said. "There are many trails we can take with the quads and there will be other foot patrols walking the park. If we haven't seen anything by noon, we're going to bring in a pair of choppers to do a flyover."

"Is that really necessary?" Morris asked. "We have a lot of campers out and about today. We don't need to spoil their day with helicopters flying around."

"If we haven't found them," Officer Smith said, "then it's very necessary. We'll keep you informed on our progress. If you hear anything let us know."

"We will officer," Morris said.

The officers got on their ATVs and took off. Morris, Lacey, and Brandi didn't say a word. They watched the officers disappear over a hill. They all knew what may have happened, although none of them wanted to say anything.

"We need to get out the map," Brandi said.

The group quickly made their way on Morris's ATV to the main office. The trio rushed in, got to a back room, and closed the door. Morris pulled an old large map from a drawer as Lacey and Brandi moved some random items off a wooden table. Morris set the map down and the group looked over the map, which was the same map that Greg had found in the library.

"I don't know how they found that trail," Morris said. "When something is hidden, why do people go looking for it?"

"It's human nature," Brandi said. "There are so many people who know the damn legends, have heard rumors about it, and I suppose a group of college kids who want one last hurrah think finding a hidden trail would be fun. The main question is, did these kids find the first base camp or are they higher in the hills by now?"

"I'm sure if they did go on the trails," Morris said. "The girls would have been at the base camp. I bet that's where they spent the night, they had tents with them."

"I wonder if they went higher into the hills and found the logging site?" Lacey asked.

"If they did," Brandi said. "We can bet they would take the northeast trail to try and get higher into the hills. If they did they did that, it would take them right into the trap."

"There would be no helping them," Morris said. "There's nothing we can do. We can't catch up to them on foot and there's no way we could get an ATV that far into the hills."

"Lacey and I could take kayaks," Brandi said. "We could make it to the campsite and try to stop them before they get further."

"Even if you were able to make it to the campsite," Morris said. "I'm sure they've already left this morning. They wouldn't want to waste time. They'd be too far ahead for you to catch on foot from the base camp, even if we knew for sure what trail they took."

"Then what are we supposed to do?" Brandi asked. "You know, I hate this job. I hate being almost thirty, still a lifeguard, getting hit on by bozos who think that I'm just a bimbo 'cause I'm working here. I want to have a life."

"You gave that up," Lacey said. "We all gave that up when we found the shadows. They charged us with this. The shadows wouldn't take too kindly to you saying that."

"I don't care," Brandi said. "I say we get them and get the hell out of here...or better yet, leave them and we go. They couldn't follow us."

"We don't know that," Morris said. "We don't know what they could do."

"I just can't take it," Brandi said. "I've been a lifeguard here for fourteen years. I need to move on. If I have to stay here, I may as well be dead. There's no future in this."

"Don't say that, Brandi," Lacey pleaded. "Please don't say that. You know what will happen if you keep saying that."

"I don't care," Brandi said. "This has to change. It's not my fault. You were the one that wanted to search it out. You know what will happen though, right? Once we get too old the shadows will replace us. They might even replace us with the kids up there right now."

"That won't happen," Morris said. "You need to look at the big picture here."

"I am," Brandi said. "I'm taking the kayak up the river. If I can't save them, I'm going down stream and I'm not stopping until I'm far away. I know that I can do better than here."

Brandi stormed out of the room. Morris just watched her leave without saying a word. He knew that this was a bad idea and that she needed to be stopped, but he also knew that she wouldn't listen to him.

"We should try to stop her," Morris said.

"I don't think we can," Lacey said. "She's determined to get out of here—has been for a long time. Just let her go."

"We can't," Morris said. "You go out there and try to talk some sense into her. If she insists on heading up the river, you need to go with her to make sure she comes back."

"Okay," Lacey said. "I'll help her."

Lacey rushed out the door and ran towards the mouth of the river. When she got there, Brandi had stripped down to the lifeguard suit she was wearing underneath her tee shirt and shorts. She was carrying a kayak from a rack and in the process of placing it in the water. Lacey rushed up to her.

"Give me a minute," Lacey said. "I'm going to put my suit on, grab some water bottles, and a smaller map. You know how confusing those trails can be. We need to be careful."

"You've got five minutes," Brandi said. "Then I'm heading up the river."

"Five minutes," Lacey said rushing away.

Four minutes later, Lacey rushed back wearing only a black swimming suit and matching aqua socks. She had a small, insulated bag with water, and a map. Lacey grabbed a kayak and a paddle off a rack of boats for rent and brought it to the water. The women started up the river, moving at a quick pace, Brandi leading the way. They needed to use all their strength to fight their way up river, especially where there were rapids. More than once the girls had to get out of the water and carry the kayaks upstream.

It was almost an hour before they reached their first stop. Lacey and Brandi shored the boats and rushed down a small trail for about five minutes before they came to a small clearing that had a fire pit with logs set up as seating around it. They silently looked around the site for a moment before Brandi broke the silence.

"You can't make me go back," Brandi said. "I can't live like this."

"You have to stop talking like that, Brandi," Lacey said. "You know what will happen. You think it's bad now? Just wait until the shadows hear you talk like that."

"They won't hear me," Brandi said. "They can't leave the forest, I can. They won't be able to track me, won't be able to find me. I can get away from here. Once I tell those kids what they are in for, they'll take me with them. They can help me get away from here."

"First, we have to find them," Lacey said. "And it looks like that's going to be harder than we thought."

"This is only the first spot," Brandi said. "There are many other place they could be."

"What do you think that you'll do once you get out of here Brandi?" Lacey asked. "Who would take you in? Where would you work? You have no idea. We should just go back and forget that this whole conversation ever took place."

"I'm not doing that," Brandi said. "No way."

"Fine," Lacey said looking around the grounds. "They were never here. They didn't stop at this site. Let's move further up the river."

"You're not going to try and talk me out of this?" Brandi asked walking up to Lacey.

Lacey couldn't help but stare at Brandi. Lacey stood a good eight inches taller and had a good weight advantage. Lacey couldn't believe what Brandi was trying to do and couldn't imagine why she was trying to get in her face. Lacey knew what she needed to do.

"I won't try and talk you out of it anymore," Lacey said. "But we're getting behind. We know they will be rushing this morning. We need to move."

"Agreed," Brandi said turning back toward the river.

Lacey grabbed a three-foot log that was about two inches in diameter. She swung hard, connecting with Brandi's head in a sickening thud. Brandi fell to the ground out cold. Lacey picked her up and carried her to a tree in the campsite. Lacey set Brandi down then opened the pack she'd taken with her. Inside was a couple of ropes.

Lacey lifted Brandi up and tied her hands and feet to the tree. Brandi had her arms extended up as far as they could go and her feet were slightly off the ground. Lacey looked at her for a moment before slapping her in the face lightly until Brandi woke up.

"What the hell are you doing?" Brandi yelled. "You bitch! Let me down."

"You know better than to talk the way you did Brandi," Lacey said. "You know that the shadows were very specific in their instructions to us. You know that this is the only thing I could do to you."

As Brandi struggled to break free, Lacey bent down and took Brandi's aqua socks off. Lacey used the swimming footwear to smack Brandi.

"You bitch," Brandi said again as she struggled.

"I've wanted to do that for a long time," Lacey said. "I knew that you were weak and couldn't handle this. You should have stayed away, but now you'll never leave."

"Just let me go, Lacey," Brandi said. "There's no need for this. I'll be good from here on out. I won't try to run away again. Don't leave me here."

"You are stuck here, Brandi," Lacey said. "I'm sure the shadows will have much to speak with you about, or maybe they'll just kill you for you trying to run. Either way, I need to make sure they know that I am on their side. I'm sorry, I really am, but I didn't have any choice."

"No Lacey," Brandi said. "Please don't leave. I'll do anything for you. I'll be good! Please Lacey, don't leave me!"

Lacey was already out of sight as Brandi started screaming. Lacey got back to the kayaks and she pushed Brandi's into the water and watched it float down the river back towards the main beach. Lacey could hear her friend screaming as she got into her kayak and slowly started back. As Lacey paddled down the river, she tried to push out the thoughts of what would happen to Brandi. She knew that the shadows wouldn't get to her until nightfall, but then, the terror would begin.

Chapter 8

Morning's light didn't come soon enough for some of the women, but it came far too soon for the others. Savannah stood her watch and stayed awake with Roxy while she did her too. Savannah said that Jennifer didn't need to have a shift, worrying about the state of mind that she was in. As the sun broke over the horizon, they stirred in their tents. Heidi gave them rations of beef jerky, granola bars, trail mix, and water. The women ate in silence.

"Anything happen last night?" Jennifer broke the extended silence. "Did anyone see anything?"

"Nothing happened," Leah said quickly, glancing at Savannah.

"That's not true," Savannah said. "We did see something."

"Are we really going to tell them about it?" Leah asked. "They don't need to know."

"Know what?" Roxy asked.

"We saw four shadows in the night," Savannah said. "They were big shadows, bigger than teenage girls who wandered from their camp, bigger than our guys..." Savannah trailed off. Roxy's eyes were huge and she was shaking. Jennifer seemed almost indifferent to the story. Heidi was confused. She ate a handful of trail mix while she contemplated what Savannah said.

"Did you try to make contact with them?" Heidi asked.

"No," Savannah said.

"Why not?" Heidi asked. "They could have helped up. You really should have let us know right away and we all should have followed them."

"Look Heidi," Savannah said. "There were four big figures. Shadows that we couldn't identify. They were looking for something and we don't know what that something was."

"And we won't know because you didn't ask them," Heidi said. "You had no right to let us sleep while we could have been in danger. You should have followed them or at least tried to figure out what they wanted. If they were here, they must know where we are. They didn't do anything. You should have talked to them."

"Heidi," Savannah said, "they didn't bother us and I wanted to keep it that way. My only goal here is to keep you guys safe and to find our guys. Everything I'm doing out here is to those ends. You have to trust me."

"You say that a lot," Heidi said. "When are we going to get some results?"

"We will find them," Savannah said.

"I have to be back on campus tonight," Heidi said. "There's no way around it. I have a test tomorrow and we all have finals that we need to study for."

"She's right, Savannah," Jennifer said. "We need to speed this up."

"Fine," Savannah said. "Finish eating and pack up camp. We move out."

"Why are we packing up?" Roxy asked. "What if the guys come back?"

"They want speed," Savannah said. "Unless we are leaving all this stuff here we need to take it. There will be quicker paths back to the main park so we won't be coming this way."

"Whatever," Jennifer said. "We just need more speed."

"Fine," Savannah said. "Leah, come with me, we need to check the trails for which way to go next. The rest of you, pack up the camp. Leave no trace that we were here."

Savannah and Leah walked towards the edge of the trees as the others started to pack up camp. Heidi and Jennifer rolled up one of the tents and Jennifer knew if she was going to get some people to follow her, now would be the time to do it.

"You're right though," Jennifer said. "Savannah has no right to be treating us like she does. She's hurting our efforts, I think."

"I don't know," Heidi said. "I'm just in a bad mood, thinking about all the work I have to do when we get back. At this rate I won't be able to sleep tonight, just a massive study cramming session."

"But the way she's talking to us," Jennifer said, "and what else has she kept from us? How many other monsters have we not known about because of her?"

"What do you want to do about it?" Heidi asked.

"We should split up," Jennifer said. "We can cover more ground and be more spread out. You and I, maybe Roxy too, should take one trail. Savannah and Leah can take a different one."

"Both Savannah and Leah are athletic," Heidi said. "Both are tough. We should have one of them in each group, just in case. Make it Savannah and Roxy, Leah coming with us."

"You and I work out," Jennifer said. "We can handle ourselves. I'm not worried about it. Savannah and Leah wouldn't split up anyway, they're too close with each other."

"You sure they'll let us split up?" Heidi asked. "Savannah might just follow us."

"I don't know," Jennifer said. "Whatever trail Savannah wants to take, we're going to take the opposite. Let's go tell Roxy and get her on our side."

Savannah and Leah weren't paying attention to the others as they were looking at the area where they saw the shadows the night before. Savannah was stunned, even afraid, of the fact that there were no prints, no tracks, and no traces, of anything there. There wasn't even a broken twig or bent blade of grass. In all her years of hunting, Savannah had never seen anything like that. She knew that there was something there, but couldn't believe that they didn't leave a trace.

"What do you make of this?" Leah asked.

"Damned if I know," Savannah said. "I've never encountered anything that doesn't leave a track. I think we should stick with the original plan that I had, search the next trail."

"What do we tell the others?" Leah asked.

"Tell them the truth," Savannah said. "They are going to think that I was drinking with you and we made the whole thing up, but so be it."

"Maybe we should call the rangers," Leah said. "Let them know what's going on."

"We can't," Savannah said. "I made a rash decision yesterday."

"What's that?" Leah asked.

"I inferred that the guys were smoking weed up here," Savannah said. "I said we didn't want the police to find them because it would mess up their professional lives."

"Why did you do that?" Leah asked.

"I thought we could find them," Savannah said. "The police aren't going to be looking here. The police will be on the main trails. They could get in trouble for going off the main trails. I had to act and came up with a story that would make sense. It wasn't the best story but it bought us time."

"I guess you're right," Leah said. "The police will never find them, not out on the trails that they were on. Have the rangers tried to contact us yet this morning?"

"I turned the radio off," Savannah said. "I didn't want a communication to come on and give away our position. I don't think we can go to them anyway. I doubt that Morris and Lacey know about these trails anyway."

"I don't know," Leah said. "I bet they do. Brandi doesn't know."

"Brandi doesn't know anything," Savannah said. "Can we not talk about her? We need to get back to the others and tell them the plan."

Savannah and Leah walked back to the others as they were finishing putting the last of the camping gear into the bags. The girls all picked up a bag and started for the trails. Savannah walked towards the one she'd decided on, but noticed that Heidi was leading Jennifer and Roxy to a different trail.

"What are you doing?" Savannah asked.

"We have to take this trail," Heidi said. "This is the trail they took. I'm sure of it."

"There are no recent tracks on that trail," Savannah said. "This trail has tracks, fresh tracks. It could be our guys. There's nothing that way."

"Then you go your way," Heidi said. "And we'll go ours. We can cover more ground this way and find them quicker."

"We need to stay together," Savannah said. "Above all else, if we separate now we will be putting ourselves in danger. You don't know what's out there."

"Our friends are out there," Heidi snapped back. "And you don't seem too excited to locate them. We are splitting up."

"So you're in charge now?" Savannah laughed. "Who voted on that?"

"No one voted," Heidi said. "We are just going to do what is best for the guys."

"That's not what's best for them," Savannah said. "We need to stick together."

"We're taking that trail," Heidi said. "You can do what's best for the guys and take the other trail or you can be the coward that I know you are and come with us because you're afraid to go by yourself."

"Where is this coming from?" Savannah asked. "Heidi, what's going on? What's your problem?"

"I'm just sick of you always bossing us around," Heidi said. "Just because you're an Amazon who can beat us up doesn't give you the right to push us around."

"That makes no sense," Leah said. "She never pushes us around. Someone had to take command of this trip. We need to be strong together."

"I've said what I've said," Heidi said. "We're going this way."

Heidi, Jennifer, and Roxy started walking down the trail. Leah looked towards Savannah then back to the others. Savannah stood stone faced. Leah could tell that Savannah was hurt. When the others were far enough down the trail that they couldn't see them, Savannah started crying softly. Leah hugged her.

"What's wrong?" Leah asked.

"Nothing," Savannah said, quickly drying her eyes and composing herself. "That hurt, it really did. I never thought that they would do that to me. I wonder what got into Heidi? That was so unlike her."

"What do we do?" Leah asked.

"We go down the trail that I wanted to," Savannah said. "If they paid attention to the map at all they would know that about two miles up the hills these two trails come together. It was always my plan to walk up one and back the other."

"You said we wouldn't be coming back through here," Leah said. "That's why we had to pack up."

"That's if we found them," Savannah said. "There are faster trails to get back to the main part of the park. One thing with the guys, they never really packed enough food or water. They were always bumming off us, remember? There's a good chance they need help. That's why we needed to stick together."

"What if we don't find them on either of these trails?" Leah asked.

"Then they're off-trail in the woods," Savannah said. "If that's the case, I doubt that we could do anything for them anyway."

"What if they get lost?" Leah said. "Or we get lost? There's so many reasons that we should have stayed together."

"I know," Savannah said. "You feeling up for a run?"

"Yeah why?"

"This trail is a lot longer," Savannah said. "We'll need to run to beat them to the where the trails come together."

"I'm ready," Leah said. Savannah nodded as she took off. Leah followed, pushing herself hard to keep up with Savannah's long strides. The pair ran hard for a solid ten minutes before slowing to a hard jogging pace. Both girls were dripping with sweat, but were in good enough shape to keep going. Savannah was glad that the trail was wide and smooth enough that they could run without worrying too much about injuries.

Savannah tried to look for any signs that the guys had come through here. There were a number of spots that Savannah wanted to stop and examine, but they had to keep moving. The animals, when they heard the girls' heavy footsteps, cleared out of the path. Savannah and Leah were making great time when they saw something that made them stop.

Off the trail to the left, set in the trees, was the remains of a camp. The girls quickly walked to it and looked around. There was a fire pit, makeshift shelter, and logs set as benches. Savannah pulled her gun out and slowly stepped forward. She didn't like this situation one bit.

"What do you think it is?" Leah asked.

"What is the problem here?" Savannah asked. "It's the same problem that was with the other campsite, the one we stayed at. I didn't say anything because I didn't want to upset Roxy or Jennifer. Heidi could handle it and I know you can. What's wrong here?"

"I don't know," Leah said looking around.

"Both these sites were mowed," Savannah said. "Someone's taking care of these sites."

"What do you mean?" Leah asked.

"These campsites are being maintained," Savannah said. "These trails aren't abandoned. If they were, no one would be mowing them."

"What do we do?" Leah asked.

"We need to search this site," Savannah said. "Look around and see if you can find anything that would indicate that the guys were here."

Leah and Savannah walked into the clearing and began investigating. Savannah went to the shelter. It was simple sticks with larger leaves and grasses to keep rain or sun off a person. To Savannah, it looked like the shelter was either built by someone who didn't know what they were doing or by someone who was in a hurry. There was nothing inside the shelter that would indicate that someone had been living in it or even using it.

Savannah moved away from the shelter and to the fire pit. The pit had ashes in it but hadn't been used in a long time. There had only been logs burned in it. There wasn't any firewood nearby to indicate whether someone was planning to use the site soon. Savannah realized that there was no tracks, no modern items, not even any trash to indicate that someone was recently here.

Savannah motioned Leah over to her and pulled out bottles of water. Both girls were drenched in sweat from the heat of the day. They drank the water and looked over the site.

"Nothing here," Leah said.

"I thought for sure we would find something."

"Back on the trail?" Leah asked.

Savannah nodded, pausing a second, before taking off down the trail with Leah only a step behind. They raced as fast as they could, pushing hard, hoping to meet up with the others when they reached the point where the trails met. Savannah knew that if they didn't get there first the others would take off without waiting.

As they pushed themselves as hard as they could, Savannah and Leah rounded a bend and saw Jennifer, Heidi, and Roxy standing on the trail. They were all dumbfounded, standing with wide eyes and their jaws hanging open. Savannah couldn't figure out what was so interesting. She called their names as she ran towards them but they didn't even look at her. When Savannah and Leah broke the tree line and approached their friends, they also stopped in their tracks. There, set in the forest, right on the river, was an abandoned city.

Chapter 9

The girls stood in awe as they gazed at the town before them. None of them could have ever imagined that something this mysterious would be hidden deep within the foothills of their beloved state park. Each one of their minds was blank, trying to process the information before them. They couldn't really comprehend what they saw.

The clearing in the foothills where the town sat was large and square, about twenty acres total before giving back to the trees. The western edge was the river, but there appeared to be no remains of piers or docks. The town itself was falling apart. Around one hundred buildings and houses lined the gravel and grass covered streets.

The main street was wider than all the others and lined with only business looking buildings. The largest building was in the middle of the town. It had a large clock on the second story, and a partially worn out sign that indicated the building was the town hall, but the name of the city had been removed from the sign. Next to the town hall was a church. The foundation and first four feet of the walls was stone, the rest wood. It also had an amazing stone bell tower.

The yards of the houses were very small, the houses almost touched each other. Each house was very similar: one story rambler styled, very basic and practical, all in need of repairs and paint. Many had roofs that were caved in or crumbling. Very few of them had windows left and each one had an outhouse set behind it.

There were a number of horse barns set on the outskirts of the town. Every business along the main street had a hitching post outside. There were wagon ruts in the streets and some broken down wagons. On the northern edge of town was a cemetery surrounded by a vine-covered fence.

"What the hell is this place?" Jennifer asked.

"I bet this is what the guys found," Savannah said. "I bet they were investigating this. They should still be here somewhere, maybe injured or lost, but I bet they are here."

"We're gonna search the ghost town?" Roxy asked. "We should just leave."

"We need to wait a moment," Savannah said. "There's a number of things that aren't right here. This just doesn't make sense."

"Like how it looks like the grounds have been maintained?" Leah asked. "But yet all the buildings are falling down?"

"That's a good observation," Savannah said. "There are some other things. I can see from here that the city name on both the church and town hall have been erased, not by time but by human hands. Someone wanted to erase this town from history. There has to be a reason why they'd want to do something like that."

Jennifer was quiet, studying the town, looking around the area, like she was looking for something specific. Jennifer seemed to be lost deep in thought as she was looking over the town.

"Jennifer," Savannah said. "What do you think?"

"Something's wrong here," Jennifer said.

"Why do you say that?" Heidi asked.

"I've written at least a dozen research reports about this state forest and park," Jennifer said. "I've researched all aspects of this place. I've interviewed five different rangers who worked here their entire lives, one of them was almost one hundred years old, and still with it. Not a single one ever mentioned a town here. No one knew anything about it. Hell, none of them ever mentioned the logging site either. This is wrong on many different levels. We're still in the state forest limits. Someone should have known."

"What difference does the research make?" Roxy asked. "It wasn't listed anywhere."

"This town could support about a couple hundred people I would guess," Savannah said. "For a town that sized there should have been town charters, records, a register, some form of paperwork. They have a town hall here so the city has to be registered with the state, and that fact that it's within the park's boundaries means that there has to be something about it."

"But that's just it," Jennifer said. "There was nothing about it. No one said anything, no record contained any information."

"Maybe we should just go," Roxy said. "This place was abandoned for a reason, we should respect that and just walk away."

"The guys found this place," Savannah said. "I'm sure they did. They must have been here to investigate it. We need to search this town over to see if they left anything here."

"The tents were gone," Roxy said. "Maybe they went home. They could have packed up and just left, as a joke to us."

"They wouldn't have done that Roxy," Jennifer said. "Mike wouldn't have done that to me. We have to find them. I don't care about anything else at this point. Mike is my everything. I have to find him." Jennifer started to break down crying. "We have to find him. I have to have Mike by my side."

"We'll find him, Jennifer," Savannah said. "We need to assess the situation here. There's an abandoned town that no one seems to know about. From what we can tell, between the facts that there's no records of the town and that the name was destroyed from the signs leads me to believe that something happened here."

"Happened here?" Roxy asked. "What do you mean?"

"I don't know yet," Savannah said. "My biggest problem here is there's no reason for a town here."

"What do you mean?" Heidi asked.

"Towns were built for strategic reasons," Savannah said starting to pace. "They were either built on navigable rivers or around railroad stations. This location doesn't make sense. It could have been a rally point for the logging site, and I would be willing to bet there's more logging sites in the woods, but there's no mill here, no lumber yard."

"We haven't even been in the buildings yet," Heidi said. "How in the world do you know that there's no mill here?"

"There would be racks," Savannah said, "to hold the finished wood. There would be channels or some kind of tracks to get the logs from the river to the mill. Another problem is that this town is upstream from the logging site. They aren't going to move those logs up river."

"What if there's gold in the hills?" Jennifer asked. "This could be a gold town, maybe other resources."

"How many reports have you done on this park?" Savannah asked.

"At least a dozen," Jennifer said.

"And did you come across any information on mining?" Savannah asked. "Any wealth created by gold or silver?"

"None," Jennifer said.

"Then I doubt that there's gold there," Savannah said. "Come on. We're going into the church to climb the bell tower. We can get a better look at the town and see what we're up against."

"Climb the tower?" Heidi asked. "Are you sure it's safe?"

"It's stone," Savannah said. "If the masons who built it had any skill at all, it'll stand for another couple hundred years. We need to scan the area, see if we can see any sign of the guys. Keep your eyes open for anything that looks modern, out of place, or just strange."

"The whole place is strange," Leah said taking a small nip from her flask. "Strange is somewhat of a relative term at this point."

"I'll grant you that," Savannah said. "Follow me. Stay close."

Savannah pulled her handgun out and kept it at the ready as she and the group slowly made their way to the church. They kept their eyes open, scanning all of the area, looking for anything that would indicate that the guys had been there. As they got to the church, Savannah motioned the others to stay at the bottom of the steps while she climbed to the heavy wooden doors. Savannah knocked loudly on the door.

"Really?" Heidi said. "You're going to knock?"

"If someone's in there," Savannah said. "We don't want to sneak up and startle them. Leah, Heidi, open the doors, keep yourselves behind them."

Leah and Heidi went to the double doors while Savannah stood in the middle of the doors, safety off, aimed right at the doors. Savannah nodded. The women opened the doors and nothing came out, nothing was inside. The entrance of the church was stone, and it appeared that no one had been inside for many years.

Savannah made her way in first, looking over the stone. There was a coatroom to her right, basement stairs to her left, and the main worship hall in front of them. She could see that there had been wooden pews in the church that were mainly rotted away. Near the entrance for the basement stairs was a doorway. The door was on the ground and nearly submitted to time. Savannah could see that the hallway led to the spire stairs.

Savannah motioned the others to follow her up the stone stairs in the spire. They slowly made their way up, the stone steps were starting to crumble, but were still firm enough to support the weight of the girls. As the girls made it to the top, Savannah motioned them to stay on the stairs while she checked to make sure the platform was firm enough for them to all stand on. When Savannah was confident they could all be up there, she waved them up.

The women were silent for a moment as they looked out over the forest. The spire was taller than all of the trees so they could see for a long ways. The forest looked beyond beautiful, in the vibrant greens of the new spring. Savannah looked around the city with a critical eye. She was trying to see any evidence that the guys had been there. The girls soaked up the beauty of the forest before they began to look around the city.

"This place is so amazing," Heidi said. "I would so love to live in a place like this."

"It would be nice," Savannah said. "But keep your mind on the task at hand. Do any of you see anything that looks out of place from up here?"

"There's nothing," Jennifer said almost crying. "No signs of them. Mike! Mike!"

"Don't yell," Roxy said. "Someone might hear us."

"That's the point," Jennifer said. "Mike! Mike!"

"But what if there's crazy people here?" Roxy asked.

"Then we'll fit right in with them," Savannah said. "Leah, Heidi, notice anything?"

"I'm looking at the houses," Leah said. "I'm not seeing any movement. Even in the houses with the windows, there's nothing there."

"Yeah," Heidi said. "I don't see anything strange, other than, you know, a nameless city."

"There has to be something," Savannah said. "I don't believe a city could be erased from time. There would have to be a reason, something that would cause people to abandon it."

"Like tainted water?" Roxy asked. "Or bad air or something?"

"Could be," Savannah said.

"But if that happened," Heidi asked. "Wouldn't there be dead bodies around?"

"No," Savannah said. "Animals would have eaten them by now."

"Really?" Roxy asked.

"It could have happened," Savannah said. "But then there would be no reason to erase the town. It's interesting really, like the town never grew up. It was founded, started running, it's obvious that it was expanded after it was started, but then it just petered out and died."

"How is that interesting?" Roxy asked.

"Interesting that we end up here, now at this time," Savannah said. "None of us want to grow up, none of us want to move past college. We're all on the edge of the beginning of our lives, ready to jump, but none of us want to."

"The real world is overrated," Roxy said. "That's why I'm going to grad school right away. I don't want to be out in that jungle."

"I think you're making a mistake," Heidi said.

"Why?" Roxy asked.

"You don't even know if you like that field yet," Heidi said. "You don't know if you'll like the jobs out there, but yet you are spending so much time and money on pursuing it."

"Daddy's paying the bills as long as I'm in college," Roxy said.

"That's the saddest thing I've ever heard," Savannah said. "I've had to stand on my own since I was a kid. But the point is valid, we don't want to grow up and here we are."

"Were the guys here?" Jennifer asked. "That's all I care about right now."

"We will find him. They have to be here somewhere," Savannah said.

"There was the logging site," Heidi said. "How many others could there be? How many could the guys have found? We could be out here for days, looking over trails, finding sites within the forest. I say we come clean. Call the ranger station and tell them where the guys were going and let them search it out. We need to get back to campus."

"She's right," Roxy said. "There's stuff we need to do before the end of the year. There are reports due and tests coming up."

"Okay," Savannah said trying to think. "We need to check a couple more spots here then we can go back to the ranger's station and tell them what really happened. The police can search them out and the guys will have to deal with the consequences."

"We can't leave without them," Jennifer said. "We have to find them. I'm not leaving here until we have found them. Will anyone stay with me?"

"I will," Savannah said quickly. "I will stay. I finished all my work so I only need to be back for finals."

"I can stay too," Leah said. "I have everything in order."

"I have to go," Roxy said.

"Then you two can go," Savannah said. "Once we do some more searching."

"What else are we going to search?" Roxy asked.

"We are going to go through all the buildings," Savannah said. "The stores, the town hall, the barns, and the larger houses. We need to see if the guys set up a base or camp in the area, if they were here, and what else is around."

"Okay," Roxy said. "We can stick around for a couple more hours."

"What are we going to investigate first?" Heidi asked.

"The first thing we are going to do," Savannah said, "is talk to the dead."

Chapter 10

The women stood in the cemetery on the north edge of the town, looking over all the headstones. They were unsure of Savannah's plan at first, but when they realized she wanted to look over the headstones to get dates and possibly a name of the town it started to make sense. The stones were all very old and worn, but they were still able to read most of them.

"This one died 1891," Savannah said. "These stones are all from about 1875 to 1895."

"I don't see anything newer than 1897 here," Heidi said. "What does that all mean? This place was only used for twenty-five or thirty years?"

"This town could have only been used for a short amount of time," Savannah said. "Who knows how it was founded or started, what the reasons were."

"I don't know if you guys realize this," Leah said looking over the stones, "but there's a lot of people here who died on August 4th, 1893. I've noticed at least seven graves that have that date on them."

"Sounds like something did happen here," Savannah said. "I wonder what. Do any of these graves have any indication of the name of the town?"

"Nope," Heidi said.

They continued looking over the stones, trying to find any clue as to what happened. Savannah carefully read them hoping for some clue, but nothing came up. Savannah noticed that Roxy had been standing in front of one of the markers the entire time and was crying. Savannah walked over and put her arm around Roxy.

"What's going on, girl?" Savannah asked.

"These two girls were twins," Roxy said. "They were only a few hours old when they died."

"The stone says they were baptized before they died," Savannah said. "They were survived by their parents and big brother. They died peacefully, Roxy."

"Oh," Roxy said crying harder. "You read that? What language is it?"

"Latin," Savannah said. "I learned in middle school."

"I'm so bad at things like this," Roxy said turning to cry on Savannah's shoulder. "I wish I was like you, not having any emotions. It would make things so much easier. I cry all the time. I can't control it."

"I'm not devoid of emotions," Savannah said. "I just hide them well. It's not all it's cracked up to be. There are times where I wish I could cry."

"Promise me one thing," Roxy said.

"What's that?" Savannah asked.

"When you need to cry you use my shoulder," Roxy said.

"I will," Savannah said. Roxy hugged Savannah before turning and walking around more headstones.

As Savannah looked around, she noticed that there were shadows moving around the edge of the forest. She couldn't see anything specific, but she could see the flicker of movement in the trees. Savannah was trying to get a better look when Leah walked up to her.

"You really know Latin?" Leah asked.

"Hell no," Savannah said. "I just told her what she needed to hear."

"Smart," Leah said. "We're being watched."

"I know."

"From the north."

"All sides. Even on the other side of the river."

"What does it mean?" Leah asked. "It looks to be the same figures we saw last night. They move enough that we can see them, but they won't step into the light."

"That's what they want."

"What do you mean?"

"They've exposed their position to us," Savannah said. "They want us to know that they are watching us. They are gathering intelligence about our position and defense. They want to know how armed we are, how we are moving, and our reasons are for being here."

"They've gotta know that we're under armed and in the middle of nowhere," Leah said. "They can take us. Why are they waiting?"

"They are not here to kill us," Savannah said.

"How do you know that?" Leah asked.

"If they were going to kill us," Savannah said, "they would have done it. They could have wiped all of us out without a challenge last night. They only looked at what was going on. They might be trying to scare us into leaving."

"Is it working?" Leah asked.

"Not really," Savannah said handing Leah the gun. "Cover me. I want to try something."

Leah took the gun as Savannah took off towards the trees. The shadows seemed to move more as she got closer. When Savannah was a few feet away from the trees, the shadows disappeared. Savannah looked back towards the group and realized that they were all looking at her. Savannah jogged back to them.

"What were you doing over there?" Heidi asked.

"Thought I saw something," Savannah replied.

"Why didn't you take the gun with you?" Roxy asked as Savannah took the gun back from Leah. "You should have been armed going out like that."

"I thought if someone was watching us," Savannah said, "that they would run if I approached with a gun in my hand. I told Leah to cover me."

"What was out there?" Jennifer asked.

"Nothing," Savannah said. "There was nothing out there. I must have been seeing shadows. Have you guys found anything here that helps us at all?" Everyone shook their heads no. They seemed a bit dejected. Savannah breathed a heavy sigh as she looked around the area.

"What's the next move?" Jennifer asked.

"We need to search the buildings," Savannah said. "We need to find out what was going on and whether the guys were here. There has to be some indication."

"I don't know, Savannah," Heidi said. "This trip has been a bust. There's been nothing here. We've found nothing. I think it's time to pack it in."

"If you and Roxy want to hike back and go, then go," Savannah said. "No one here will judge you for it. We need to find out what's going on here."

"Please stay for a little longer," Jennifer pleaded. "I need you guys to stay with me. We need to have as many people here as we can."

"Okay," Heidi said wiping her brow. "Does it really need to be this hot here? It's like the gates of hell have been opened."

"It is strange," Jennifer said. "What's the plan, Savannah? What do we do now?"

"We'll split up now: Leah with me and the three of you together. We'll be going into buildings right next to each other, so there shouldn't be too much danger. I'll hang onto the gun. Remember, if you holler for us, I'll be running in with the gun ready to fire and I don't hesitate in hostile situations."

"Okay," Heidi said. "What buildings are we searching first?" Savannah motioned for the others to follow her. She walked down the street until she got to what looked like a hardware store. Next door was a building, more similar to a barn, with the markings of a blacksmith's shop. Savannah motioned towards the hardware store.

"You three take the hardware store," Savannah said. "Look for an abundance of certain items that would indicate what they were doing here."

"What do you mean by that?" Heidi asked.

"If there's saws and axes," Savannah, "that means this was a logging town. Shovels and picks would mean that they were mining for something. Plows and scythes would mean that this was a farming town. Stuff like that. Also see if there's anything that looks like it's been recently taken, something that's been moved."

"How could we tell if it's been moved?" Roxy asked.

"There will be a lot of dust on everything," Savannah said. "Look at the dust and the surrounding items, see if they match. Leah and I will be the blacksmith shop. If you come to get us, make sure to announce yourselves; don't sneak up on me."

"Okay," Heidi said. Jennifer and Roxy followed Heidi into the hardware store. Once they were inside, the shadows that had been playing in the tree lines came back. Both Savannah and Leah could see them there. They watched the shadows dance for a moment.

"Just as I expected," Savannah said. "At first I thought that the shadows disappeared because I was walking towards them, but it was because Jennifer looked at them. For some reason they only want us to see them."

"That makes no sense," Leah said. "None of this makes any damn sense."

"I know," Savannah said. "There's something wrong with this town. You notice how it felt like it got about ten degrees hotter when we entered the town?"

"I thought that was just in my head," Leah said. "This is too freaky. Maybe we should just get out of here."

"I don't know," Savannah said. "At first, I thought that the guys may have been pranking us. You know, not show up, don't answer their phones, and then we show up here and they jump out and scare the piss out of us."

"You waiting for them to jump out?" Leah asked.

"I don't know anymore," Savannah said. "I think that they're in danger. Something is wrong. If someone was injured, they could have sent one person to get help. They shouldn't have been silent this long. I'm not sure what we should do at this point."

"You think searching the buildings is moot?" Leah asked.

"No," Savannah said. "We need to get in there and see what is going on. I'm sure that the guys were here, somewhere in this town. Maybe its intuition, I don't know, but the guys were here. Come on."

Savannah, with her gun drawn, slowly made her way into the walk-in door in the front of the barn. Leah followed closely behind her. The interior of the barn was scattered with metal. One corner of the barn had eight anvils in two rows. There was smelting equipment, a massive fire pit, hammers, benches, and all kinds of strange tools. In the middle of the barn was a broken-down wagon that was beginning to rot away.

"Must be really busy here," Savannah said. "They didn't even have time to fix an axel."

"There hasn't been anyone in this barn for years," Leah said. "There's nothing here."

"You're right," Savannah said. "But we are going to search this place anyway. Look around for anything that's been moved or for something wrong with the dust."

"There's plenty of dust here," Leah said. "Not much else though. What would they do with all this stuff? I thought blacksmiths just shoed horses."

"They did a lot more than that," Savannah said. "They would do anything with metal. These guys could make anything with metal. The blacksmith was an amazing career. Outside of the tavern, he was the busiest person in town."

"We should hit the tavern," Leah said. "I could use a drink."

"You've been doing so well today though," Savannah said. "I haven't seen you drinking at all. Why would you want to start again?"

"It's this town," Leah said. "There's something evil here. I can't describe it but there is something wrong with this town. When I saw those shadows, I knew we were in big trouble."

"Nothing has happened yet," Savannah said.

As Savannah finished talking, they heard a blood curdling scream from the building next door. Both Leah and Savannah wasted no time in rushing out the door and into the hardware store next to it. The store was filled with shelving units and the remains of items that were sitting on those shelves. They could see some basic tools but nothing to indicate that there was a certain industry in the area.

As they moved further into the store, they saw the other girls. Roxy was screaming, crying, and almost hysterical. Savannah was aiming her gun just past Roxy, ready in case there was something there, but she didn't see anything. Savannah moved closer and that's when she saw what had caused the commotion; human bones on the floor. Savannah grabbed Roxy and carried her out of the store. Everyone followed them outside.

"Pull yourself together, Roxy," Savannah said as Roxy continued to freak out.

"I can't…what the hell was that?" Roxy said through her tears.

"It was the remains of a person," Savannah said. "Nothing more than that. We were just in an entire area like that in the graveyard. No difference."

"But I saw those bones," Roxy said. "They were in front of me. Someone died there."

"I saw the bones, Roxy," Savannah said. "They were very old. They couldn't have belonged to any of our guys."

"But there was a dead person there," Roxy screamed. "Dead, just like all of us are going to be. We are going to die in this forest just like the guys did."

"No one's going to die here," Savannah said. "How do you know they died here? You don't. We don't know what happened to them, that's why we're looking for them."

"We are going to die here," Roxy said. "I know it."

"No, you don't," Savannah said. "You are better than that Roxy. Snap out of this. We are going to find them. I told you to trust me. Have I ever let you down before?"

"No," Roxy said.

"Okay," Savannah said. "Was there anything else in that store?"

"Nothing," Heidi said. "Just ruins of what used to be. Nothing to indicate that anyone was there recently. Everything was covered in dust and it didn't look like anything had been moved."

"There's a lot of buildings here," Savannah said. "I don't want to try to split up again. I need to think for a moment."

Savannah paced back and forth. She looked towards the forest and saw the shadows playing on the edge of the trees again. The shadows disappeared and Savannah realized that Jennifer had lifted her head and was looking towards the trees as well. Savannah scanned hoping to catch another glimpse of them. There was nothing though, and even when Jennifer looked away, the shadows didn't come back.

Savannah brought her mind back to the task at hand. She realized they were in a bad position. They had no indication that the guys were in the town and hadn't seen any clue as to where they were. She was at a loss at how they really should proceed. For the first time in a long time, Savannah was scared of what was going on. The others were getting impatient.

"What's the next move, Savannah?" Jennifer prodded.

"We are going to search the town hall," Savannah said. "And if we don't find anything there, we need to pack it up and leave the search to the police."

Chapter 11

The girls slowly walked down the main street and stopped when they got in front of the town hall. Savannah studied the building, something about it called her attention, but she couldn't figure out what. Savannah looked back towards the tree line to see if the shadows were back, but there was nothing there.

The Town Hall building was large, on par with the size of the church and one of the larger barns. The front was covered under a porch overhang that was supported with four pillars that were wooden and covered with carvings, most of which had given way to time. There were large, partially open double doors.

Savannah took the lead and slowly made her way up the stairs to the entrance. The others followed two paces behind her. When she got to the doors, Savannah motioned for Leah and Heidi to open them. Savannah stood in the middle with her gun raised. Leah and Heidi slowly opened the doors and Savannah found herself staring down a long hallway with many doors on both sides.

Savannah slowly made her way into the hallway and up to the first door on the right. She positioned herself outside the door while motioning the others to stay back. Savannah quickly opened the door and pointed her gun inside, finding herself in a coatroom. She smiled, laughing slightly, as she quickly scanned the small room before backing out and shutting the door.

"What was in there?" Jennifer asked.

"Nothing," Savannah said. "It was the coatroom. I'm sure there's a lot of rooms in this building. If we're lucky, there'll be records, information, about what went on here. We could find out a lot about this town."

"I don't care about the town, Savannah," Jennifer said. "We need to find the guys."

"Think for a moment, Jennifer," Savannah said. "There will be maps here and information about the area. Maybe they came through here, found something. We might be able to find out where they are at."

"All I care about is Mike," Jennifer said. "I won't give up on him."

"And neither will we," Savannah said. "We need to keep moving though."

Savannah moved across the hall to a large door with a stained glass window in it. There was a place near the door for a sign that indicated in the past what was behind the door, but the sign had succumbed to time and was no longer visible. The doors were shut tight. Savannah slowly opened the door and burst into the room, gun drawn, only to almost drop the gun when she saw what was in the room.

The room had been a waiting room. There were benches on the walls and two rows of chairs in the middle. At one end of the room, there was a window in the wall with a desk beside it. The window covered at two thirds of the opening in the wall, having a slot at the bottom that was just big enough to pass papers back and forth. The shocking part of the room was that it was freshly painted, brightly colored, and all the benches, chairs, window, and the room itself looked new.

The other girls walked into the room behind Savannah and were just as stunned. There was no explaining what they were looking at. They couldn't believe that someone would have taken the time to fix a room like this. Savannah noticed that there was another door in the room, on the same wall as the window. Savannah moved to the door and tested it, it swung open, and she went through. The other women followed her.

The room held floor to ceiling wooden filing cabinets. They covered all the walls and looked restored. There were three large wooden desks against the wall with the window and the door. Savannah noticed that the door could be barred from the inside so that no one in the waiting room could get inside. The room was fixed up and looked almost new.

"What is this?" Roxy asked. "Why would they have this here?"

"These are the town records," Savannah said. "There should be files on everyone who lived here. We need to search these files and see if we can find anything interesting about this town. Any information that we can find could be helpful. You guys start going through the cabinets. I'm going to search the desks."

They started to search the files. Savannah opened the middle drawer of the biggest desk, but there was only a ledger inside. She opened the book, but the ink had faded away many years ago. There wasn't any way to pull information from it. Savannah closed the book and put it back. She moved to the top right drawer. There were faded papers, unreadable, loosely set in the drawer. Savannah went through the rest of the drawers, finding faded papers, until she came across a paper that wasn't faded away yet. It was a record of the town annexing part of the forest.

"The town is Amber Hollow," Savannah said. "That's what this record says. Have you guys been able to find anything?"

"These are all basic records," Leah said. "Birth, death, marriage. Nothing weird."

"The only thing out of the ordinary," a female voice said from the doorway. "Is why there are five girls trespassing in my home."

The girls whipped around to look at the door. Savannah had her gun drawn, but was stunned by what she saw standing there: a teenage girl. The girl was darkly tanned, with long black hair. She was tall and thin, almost undernourished, but she seemed healthy. Everything she wore was black: her pants, tank-top, knee high boots, belt, and fingerless elbow length gloves. She had heavy black eye shadow and was hauntingly beautiful. The girl didn't flinch at all at Savannah holding a gun on her. She simply smiled as Jennifer rushed up to her.

"Have you seen Mike?" Jennifer asked frantically. "Have you seen my fiancée? He was with a group of his friends."

"I haven't," the girl said. "To be honest, I haven't seen anyone in a long time."

"What are you doing here?" Heidi asked. "Who are you?"

"I live here," the girl said. "What are you doing here?"

"We had four friends," Jennifer said, "led by my fiancée who came here to investigate the legend of the hidden trails. They were supposed to return Sunday night, but we haven't see them. We came here to try to find them."

"Heard that story before," the girl said. "In various forms. People hear the legend and they come running. Let me ask you a question, did you ever think that the trails were hidden for a reason? That maybe something up here shouldn't be found?"

"What is this place?" Leah asked.

"Amber Hollow was a town primed to capitalize on the lumber. Once the trees were logged, they figured the land would make great farmland. It was going to be a nice little community, a trading post, and a logging and farming town. It could have been a great city if it'd been given the chance to thrive."

"Why didn't it?" Leah asked.

"Lots of reasons," the girl said. "But first, how's about we start with your names."

"I'm Jennifer," Jennifer said. "This is Heidi, Leah, Roxy, and the Amazon holding the gun is Savannah."

"I'm unarmed and smaller than you, Savannah," the girl said. "You can lower the gun."

"We haven't gotten your name yet," Savannah said. "Or what you're doing here."

"My name is Melanie Larsen," Melanie said. "I live here in Amber Hollow. This is my home that you're so eagerly trespassing through."

"Your home?" Savannah asked. "How old are you?"

"Fifteen."

"Where are your parents?"

"Dead."

"Who do you live with?"

"No one," Melanie said. "I live alone here. My parents died two years ago and I had nowhere else to go. I came here. I've made a home for myself here."

"There's one problem with that story, Melanie," Savannah said. "You're too clean. Your clothes are clean. You got a washing machine sitting in here?"

"No," Melanie said with a smile. "But I do have a shower. You could use it, smells like you need one."

"There's no power here," Savannah said. "How do you have running water?"

"The windmill," Melanie said. "It pumps water. It's not warm, but it's not freezing. It's enough to keep me and my clothes clean. I have everything that I need here."

"But don't you have people who are worried about you?" Heidi asked. "Family somewhere that are concerned for your well-being?"

"I have an older sister," Melanie said. "But she doesn't care about me. She never did. I'm not even sure where she is now. There was no other family."

"How did you find this place?" Savannah asked.

"I knew about it," Melanie said. "I had relatives that lived here when Amber Hollow was a thriving town. They helped build this little village. I had read about it in a diary and I always wanted to visit. Now that I'm here, I'm the mayor. I'm in charge of the town."

"A bit young to be a mayor, aren't you?" Savannah asked.

"I can't wait to grow up," Melanie said. "I want nothing more than to be an adult so that no one can ever tell me what to do again. That's one of the things that I love about this place. I'm in charge. I make the rules. You have to do what I tell you to." Savannah raised the gun and pulled the hammer back. She had it aimed right between Melanie's eyes.

"You gonna give me an order there, sweetie?" Savannah asked. "Come on, give me an order and we'll see how well you're running this town."

"You can put that gun down," Melanie said, "and meet me face to face, no tricks, and we'll see how well you follow orders."

"Savannah, stop," Heidi said. Savannah slipped the hammer back on the gun and put the safety on before tossing the gun to Leah.

Savannah walked right up to Melanie, so close the two were almost touching. "Come on, give me an order now."

"Get on your knees and beg me for help," Melanie said. "I was going to open myself and my home up to you, help you search for your friends freely and willingly, but because you're acting like this I want you to get on your knees and beg me." Jennifer fell to her knees and held her hands together like she was praying.

"Please Melanie," Jennifer said. "Please help us find Mike and the others."

"Not from you," Melanie said. "Savannah, on your knees."

"I don't get on my knees for anyone," Savannah sneered.

"Yeah right," Melanie said with a laugh. "I bet we all believe that. I'm going to say this one more time, on your knees."

"Make me," Savannah said.

Melanie smiled before quickly snagging a paperweight off the desk swinging it at Savannah's head. Savannah tried to block, but Melanie was so quick and fluid with her movement that Savannah didn't have time to react. The weight hit Savannah's head with a sickening thud, causing Savannah to scream out in pain and fall to the floor. Savannah was on her hands and knees in front of Melanie. The others were frozen still. Leah quickly pulled the gun up on Melanie.

"Drop it," Leah said. "Drop it now."

"Okay," Melanie said dropping the weight. "Now ask me nicely, Savannah."

"Would you please help us?" Savannah asked through gritted teeth.

"Yes, I will," Melanie said offering her hand to help Savannah up. "That wasn't so hard now was it? Just remember that I'm in charge around here." Savannah took Melanie's hand and started to stand up. When she was just about standing, Savannah quickly took Melanie to the floor, locking her neck into a painful twisting hold.

"Don't ever do that again," Savannah said. "I'll take your orders, but you'd better not be jerking us off or I'm going to really get mad, okay?"

"Okay," Melanie said trying to struggle underneath Savannah. Savannah stood up, standing Melanie up with her. Savannah offered her hand for a handshake. Melanie took it.

"We've each hurt the other," Savannah said. "We're even and there's no reason to do it again. Let's just find the guys."

"Agreed," Melanie said.

"Melanie," Jennifer said. "Did you fix this place up yourself? Are you the one painting it and cleaning and what not?"

"I am," Melanie said.

"Where do you get the supplies for all of this?" Leah asked.

"The forest service," Melanie said, "doesn't keep a very close eye on inventory or accounts. I'm able to borrow everything I need from them."

"How do you borrow paint?" Heidi asked.

"I keep track of everything I use," Melanie said. "And when this town is up and running again I will pay them all back, plus interest. I'll also allow them to use this town in any capacity to help the forest or the park."

"Which house do you live in?" Savannah asked.

"I live here," Melanie said, "in the town hall. I figured that this would be the first building that I would fix up so I would be spending a lot of time here. I wanted to be close to it. I fixed up a little bedroom in a supply room. It's small, but I've got everything I need."

"Do you really think that they'll allow you to stay here?" Savannah asked. "When they find out about you, I mean. Do you think that you'll be able to stay or do you think that they'll kick you out of here?"

"That's a good question," Melanie said. "But I've been listening to you since you got here, been watching you, and you didn't even know I was around. I only made myself known when I wanted to. Had I not exposed myself, you would have never known I was here. It's the same with the rangers. They never come up here, but they've never seen me in the camp either. I do what I need to so that I can survive."

"Fine," Jennifer said. "Where can we find the guys?"

"There's a farm site," Melanie said. "Not too far from here. That would be the most logical place to start looking. It's an amazing site, lots of people who hear about the hidden trails want to find it."

"Then take us to it," Savannah said. Melanie smiled and waved them along as she started to make her way out of the town hall. The others paused for a moment before following.

Chapter 12

Melanie led the girls along a trail that followed the river north, slowly approaching the base of the mountains. The hiking was getting harder as the gentle rolling hills became steeper and higher. It didn't take them long before they were standing in the yard of an old, abandoned farm site. The site had a dilapidated house, a barn, outbuilding, and the foundations for a few other buildings. The buildings were barely standing and everything looked ready to fall apart.

Savannah raised her gun before she entered the clearing of the farmyard. She looked around, wary of possible dangers. She proceeded before the others, looking to make sure that the coast was clear. Savannah didn't like the fact that there were so many places that a person could hide or attack them from. As long as they were in the yard, surrounded by tall trees, they were in a very exposed position.

"Who use to live here?" Savannah asked.

"I don't know their names," Melanie said. "Not for certain anyway, but they had a daughter named Sophia. She was the one who wrote the diary."

"What ever happened to her?" Heidi asked.

"She shares a story similar to mine," Melanie said. "She wanted to grow up. She was tired of being a kid, having people tell her what to do, where she should go, all that kind of stuff. Her older sister was getting married. It was going to be a massive wedding, top of the line all the way. This family was the one of the larger farm in the area and they only had two daughters. The man she was marrying was the son of the largest farmer in the area. They thought that with these two getting married it would be a good unifying even for the town. Sophia didn't agree. She wanted to marry, but everyone told her she was too young."

"What happened to her?" Heidi asked.

"She ran away from home," Melanie said. "And she was never to be seen again. No one ever heard from her."

"That's strange," Savannah said. "What do they think happened to her?"

"Some think that she hiked high into the mountains where there's a cave. She would have starved to death up there. Others think that she got lost in the woods."

"Does her spirit roam the woods," Heidi asked. "Looking for young men to marry and drag to hell to be her eternal bridegroom?"

"Nothing like that," Melanie said. "I've been here two years and I haven't seen her. I'm sure she got out of the forest and ran to a town. She probably found someone to marry and lived happily ever after. It sure would be nice if that's how it really worked out."

"Would be nice, but I doubt it," Savannah said. "There's a problem here. Same problem with the other sites we were at. This place has been mowed. Who's maintaining these sites?"

"I am," Melanie replied. "Once I get this town up and running I'm going to need tourism to get some funds flowing in. I'm going to restore a lot of the historic sites around here so that there are sites to visit. I plan on fixing up the tavern-hotel next, so there's a place for people to stay. It's going to be an amazing site when I finish. People will flock from all over to see it."

"To see a ghost town," Savannah said.

"There are no ghosts there," Melanie said. "I've lived there alone for two years and have never seen a ghost there. You'd think, a teenaged girl, alone, would be a prime candidate for a haunting but sadly, no, there are no ghosts here. I was hoping there would be, that I could find a good haunted building to restore. I could have promoted this place as a ghost town, but nope, there's nothing haunted."

"This place seems ideal for a haunting," Savannah said. "Too bad. Real ghosts could have boosted your tourism."

"It really would have made this place famous," Melanie said.

"You could fake it," Leah said. "You could hire some actors, do a little work, and make it look haunted."

"Sooner or later," Melanie said. "People would discover the truth and then the place would be dead again. I doubt they would take too kindly to getting duped like that."

"You never know," Savannah said. "People like all kinds of crazy stuff. They will pay for the experience. Tell them it's fake, but let them think it's real. Tell them they are paying for the experience."

"I could," Melanie said. "But that's not the route I want to take. Come on, we need to check this place over to see if there's anything here. Jennifer and Roxy, you check the big barn. Leah and Heidi, you look over the smaller barn. Savannah and I will take the house."

"I don't think splitting up is the best idea," Savannah said. "We are stronger when we are all together. We should stay as a group."

"There's nothing here," Melanie said. "If your group of guys did end up camping in one of these buildings we need to find the location as quickly as we can. Splitting up makes sense."

"I agree with her," Jennifer said.

"As do I," Heidi said.

"That's three for splitting up." Savannah said. "I vote we stick together."

"So do I," Leah said.

"That just leaves you Roxy," Savannah said. "Do you want to split up or do you want to stick together?"

"I want to stay together," Roxy said, "it's safer that way."

"Three to three," Savannah said. "Tie. In the event of a tie, we keep doing what we were doing before, we stick together."

"We're going to split up," Melanie said walking up to Savannah. "I wouldn't want to embarrass you again by dropping you to your knees and making you beg. Just follow my lead."

Savannah glared at Melanie. One minute she would seem like a nice person, but the next she would be totally different. Savannah was no strangers to fights—soccer is a rough sport, but she didn't want to waste time out here, and she didn't think Melanie fought fair. It seemed like she had a big trick up her sleeve. Savannah tried to think as quickly as she could for a way to back away from the fight and yet not lose face with the others.

"Are you trying to destroy this group?" Savannah asked Melanie.

"No," Melanie said.

"Then why are you challenging me to a fight?" Savannah asked. "You want to wear us both out, make us tired and unprepared for what is to come? Is that what you are trying to do?"

"No," Melanie said on the defensive. "I'm not trying anything."

"You're trying to distract us from our goals," Savannah said. "You don't want us to find the guys. What, are you hoping they'll find you and you can hook up with them? Want a little action, is that your play?"

"Absolutely not," Melanie said. "You're twisting my words around. Stop doing that. We need to cover more ground. We split up."

"We're going," Jennifer said. "Come on Roxy, follow me."

Roxy and Jennifer walked towards the barn. It took a moment, but Leah and Heidi walked towards the larger barn leaving just Savannah and Melanie in a standoff. Neither wanted to back down, but neither wanted to start the fight. They just stared at each other for a moment.

"You think you're pretty tough?" Savannah asked.

"I've been in fights before," Melanie said.

"As have I," Savannah said. "I don't take kindly to people talking down to me, or trying to push me around. My only goal here is to save the guys. We don't know what your goals are or if you even have any goals. Why are you pushing me like this?"

"Think for a minute, Savannah," Melanie said. "Who knows this area better than I do? You need me as your expert if you ever want to find your friends again."

"You were quick to offer to help us, why?" Savannah asked.

"You have no idea how lonely it can be up here," Melanie said. "I wish upon ever star that I see for people to come and visit me. You seem to have taken control of the group and are working very hard to save the guys. What's your aim in all of this? You want one of them?"

"No," Savannah said. "I'm just helping my friends. My friends are all I have. There's no family, well, none that care about me. These girls are the only people who've ever loved me, treated me like an equal, and welcomed me without question."

"No one else has ever done that?" Melanie asked. "Not even in school?"

"Not like this group has," Savannah said. "I would do anything for them. Jennifer needs my help now. I have to be strong for her because she's going through so much."

"We have the same basic goals. I'll help you find them and you guys will keep me company for a short time, maybe visit once in a while. Can we just start looking around?"

"I'll follow your lead."

"Thank you," Melanie said.

Melanie led the way with Savannah and her gun behind. They made it to the old, two story farmhouse. The house was dilapidated. All the glass was broken out of the windows and the paint had faded and chipped away. Savannah was nervous about walking on the floors, wondering if the wood was strong enough to support their weight. They climbed on the porch steps, creaking along the way, and got to the front door. Melanie motioned that she was going to open the door and wanted Savannah ready with the gun.

Melanie swung the door open and Savannah aimed before slowly moving into the house. The entrance was empty, with a large hole in a wall that looked to have been made by an animal. There was nothing else though, no random items scattered about, no clothing hung on the wall hooks, no trinkets on the shelves, an empty house. Savannah moved further in, noting how unbearably hot it was inside the house. She'd figured that with no glass in the windows the house would be about the same as the outside temperature but it was at least fifteen degrees hotter inside than out.

"The house looks empty," Savannah said. "It looks like they took everything with them."

"They did," Melanie said. "There's no furniture in the rooms. It's strangely uncomfortable. It doesn't feel like a home."

"Do you want to restore this house too?" Savannah asked.

"I would like too," Melanie said. "This would be a fine place to live. That's why I keep it maintained. I have a list of the things I'd like to fix."

"How?"

"First, I'd need to make sure the structure is sound. Probably fix a couple weak spots in the floor, roof, and walls. Then shingles, windows, paint, and a number of other things like that on the outside. Inside, I would start with plumbing and electric, painting everything, putting down new flooring, and trim work and finishing touches."

"That's going to take a long time," Savannah said. "And it will be expensive."

"You think the house is bad," Melanie said, "wait until you see the barns. I'll need to put a lot more money into them. It's going to take a long time, but once I have the town up and running it shouldn't be so hard."

Savannah nodded as they walked further into the house. The floors creaked with every step. Savannah moved slowly, testing each step to make sure she didn't end up taking a quick trip to the basement. She also kept her eye on Melanie, not fully trusting her, but also not wanting to say anything. Savannah knew that she could defend herself, but Melanie didn't play by the rules. She could easily find something to strike Savannah with and that would be a quick end to any fight.

They made their way into the kitchen. There was a long, heavy table, with eight chairs around it, but nothing else. There was no refrigerator, no oven or stove, and no dishes of any kind. The facades of all the cabinets had been ripped off and they could see that all the cupboards were bare along with the pantry and other shelving. Everything in the room was exposed and there was nothing, not even a mouse in that house.

"This seems so strange," Savannah said. "There should be something here."

"If they did leave anything in a house like this," Melanie said, "I'm sure that it's been picked through before. I'm sure that anything left was stolen."

"They didn't take the table," Savannah said tapping the top of the table. "I doubt they could have gotten that very far in the forest; it's too heavy."

"If your friends had gotten to this house," Melanie said, "I doubt they would have gone up the stairs. They would have stayed here."

"Mike!" Savannah shouted. "Greg! Todd! Steve!" There was no answer.

"It's Savannah!" she shouted, but there was still no reply. "I think you're right. They're not here and there's no indication that they've been here."

"How do you know that?" Melanie asked.

"Look," Savannah said pointing down. "We are leaving footprints in the dust. They didn't leave any tracks in here."

"Good observation," Melanie said. "Are you like an investigator or something? You don't seem to miss anything."

"Accountant," Savannah said. "Let's see if the others have found anything."

Savannah and Melanie met up with the others in the middle of the yard, but the looks on their faces told the story before they said a word. No one had seen any sign of the guys. The trip to the farm had been a bust. Savannah knew that something was wrong. Melanie didn't seem completely right either. As they walked back to town, the feeling grew and grew. Savannah's instincts were going off like crazy and she couldn't figure out why. When they got back to the camp, they realized there was no way to hike out before it got dark. Heidi was furious, but agreed to stay the night before leaving right away in the morning. Melanie offered to make supper and Savannah's feelings of something being wrong got worse.

Chapter 13

The girls were impressed by the food Melanie prepared for them. Melanie stoked the fire pit outside of the town hall. She put together fresh caught fish, hare, potatoes, and even a squash. As she was cooking, the girls looked over the massive garden that Melanie tended. She already had most of it planted for the year and there were already some vegetables to harvest.

The group ate their supper in silence, no one wanting to admit that it had been far too long since they'd seen a sign of the guys. Savannah knew that by this point, they should have seen something. The fact that the tents had been packed up and moved weighed on her. She couldn't figure out why they didn't leave a note or something to indicate where they were going.

After supper, Melanie shared some moonshine with the girls. The drink was stronger than what they were used to, and it burned as they drank it down. Leah was the only one who asked for seconds and thirds. The girls settled in for what promised to be a long night, Melanie set them up in beds in the jail, with her explaining that it was the only place where there were good beds.

As the sun was setting, Savannah went over all the information they'd encountered while Jennifer, Roxy, and Heidi wandered around the town looking for more information. Only Leah remained near Melanie, the two of them sat around the fire quietly drinking.

"What's it like up here?" Leah asked. "I mean, what's it like being alone up here?"

"I've gotten used to it," Melanie said. "After everything happened, I didn't want to be around people anyway. They started to irritate me. I couldn't stand it. For the longest time, all anybody wanted to talk about was my sister's wedding and how I was a little kid who couldn't do anything. Then everyone died. I hated it really. All I wanted was to be an adult, make my own decisions, and make my own way in this world."

"I guess we sit at the opposite end of the spectrum," Leah said.

"What do you mean?"

"College is over for me," Leah said. "I have to go out into the real world, find a job, start a career, no more partying until four in the morning and going to class hung over. Everyone's going to start pushing me to settle down, get married, and have kids. I'm not ready for that. Hell, I don't want to do that. I don't think I'd make a very good mother or wife."

"You lean in different directions?"

"I've messed around," Leah said. "What college girl hasn't? But no, I would like to find a guy, but I don't want things to be so serious. I just want a couple more years of having fun."

"You can still have fun as an adult," Melanie said. "It's not like your life ends when you graduate college."

"I know," Leah said. "Want to know what my favorite college memory is? There was a party this past fall. It started on a Thursday night and lasted until Sunday evening. It was a blast. There were so many people there, and it was held in these two massive houses that were next door to each other. There were people everywhere, in the houses, in the yards, hell, even on the streets. Everyone was cool and everyone had a great time. I would love to go to parties like that all the time. Just chill out with friends, drinking, having a great time, playing some games, and just not worrying about what's coming tomorrow."

"Sounds like it was a good time," Melanie said. "But college is the time when you're supposed to get all those partying urges out of your system. You come in as a partying freshman, experience everything you want to, and by the time you're a senior, you know who you are and what you want to do with your life."

"That's not true," Leah said. "How many people switch careers or go back to get a different degree within five years of graduating? I mean, I knew girls who were seniors when I was a freshman and they're back in school again, trying to figure out a different path. The problem is that no one teaches us how to be adults. There's no class on how to grow up."

"There doesn't need to be," Melanie said. "You grow up by the experiences that you have in your life. You can't teach a person to be an adult. A person has to craft their adulthood. How are you going to start yours?"

Leah took a drink from her glass before pouring another. "You really didn't grow up."

"What do you mean?" Melanie asked. "I'm restoring a town. I'm surviving on my own."

"Yeah," Leah said, "but you hide yourself from the world. You want to be all grown up, but there's nothing to compare yourself to out here. You are still a kid who's pretending. Why did you want to grow up so fast?"

"All anyone could talk about was my stupid sister and her stupid wedding," Melanie said. "I wanted to find a man and get married but everyone said I was too young and wasn't ready. I wanted to prove them wrong. I wanted to show everyone how mature, how grown up I really was. I went out to find myself a husband. That didn't go well. Everyone makes mistakes, right?"

"What happened?"

"It's a long story."

"Looks like the fire will burn a while longer," Leah said. "And the jug of shine is still half-full. Plenty of time."

"Look," Melanie said, "I'd like to share the story with you someday, but not yet. I've let you into my home, but I'm not quite ready to let you into my heart and soul, understand?"

"I do," Leah said. "So what are your goals? What do you want out of life?"

"I'm not sure anymore," Melanie said. "I thought I could stay out here, away from all of that, but now I'm not so sure. I get so lonely up here."

"I couldn't imagine being alone this long," Leah said. "I get upset if I don't have a man keeping me company over the weekend. How long has it been since you've seen anyone?"

"It's been a long time," Melanie said. "A very long time."

"How do you handle it?"

"I guess I've fallen into a trap like you," Melanie said. "I drink. I keep myself busy. When I'm occupied, I don't tend to think about it. I have a lot of work to do here."

"You've been so nice to us," Leah said. "Is there anything we can do for you? Anyway to pay you back for what you've done?"

"I've been so lonely. I just want some companionship."

"I would need a couple more drinks," Leah chuckled. "But I can help you out. We just need to go somewhere the others won't hear us. I don't want them to know I'm still into that."

"That's not what I meant," Melanie said. "I'm talking about friends, have people to talk to, interact with. I want to be able to see people. It's going to be a long time before I have Amber Hollow ready to receive tourists. When it's up and running, I won't have any problems, but I want friends."

"I have to go back and finish school," Leah said. "But once school is over, I could come here and live with you, help you finish this place up. I'm sure things would run a lot smoother and quicker if there was an extra set of hands here helping."

"That would be great," Melanie said. "Thank you." Leah was about to respond when she noticed that the other girls were walking over to the fire. They got drinks before sitting down. They looked upset.

"I can't even call my professor," Heidi said, "to let him know I'll be late. None of the phones work up here. Why couldn't they have cell towers around the park?"

"None of the phones work here?" Leah asked.

"None," Heidi said. "This is really going to cost me."

"I have a question for you, Melanie," Savannah asked. "What really happened to this town? It seems like it was only used for a very short time before it was abandoned. Why did the people leave this town?"

"There's plenty of reasons I'm sure," Melanie said. "But there was no reason for this town. It wasn't in a strategic location. There wasn't any way to expand the town, not enough farmland for the population to grow, and nothing to hold them here."

"Has nothing to do with a curse?" Savannah asked.

"Curse?" Roxy asked swallowing in a throat suddenly dry. "There's no such thing as a curse, is there?"

"You refer to the fact that some people died here," Melanie said. "They died here on August 4th, 1893. There was an incident, not much is known about it. After that day, many people left town. The ones that stayed around slowly died off."

"How many people died that day?" Savannah asked.

"I don't know," Melanie said. "I counted around thirty graves in the cemetery with that date on it. There could have been more that aren't here."

"Something doesn't feel right about this place," Savannah said. "I can't put my finger on it but there's something wrong here. You've never found any information about that day?"

"I really haven't," Melanie said. "But then again, I haven't looked for it either. Some things need to be left in the past. I don't know what good would come from digging up bones."

"Where did you find out about this stuff, Savannah?" Leah asked.

"The dead," Savannah said. "There's a headstone that talks about the curse, which the town was built on cursed ground and it was destined to be destroyed."

"The town wasn't destroyed," Melanie said. "It's still standing tall, maybe not as shiny as before, but it's still here."

"Destroyed could mean many different things," Savannah said. "The point is, Amber Hollow is dead, a ghost town, only one person lives here and she not on any official records. The town has been hidden away in a forest to be forgotten about. That sounds destroyed to me. I'm sure the founders thought that this town would shine for the ages."

"You know more than you're letting on," Roxy said. "What else did you find out?"

"There were a lot of deaths here," Savannah said. "A week after a big wedding there was a massive amount of deaths."

"Where did you find that out?" Melanie asked.

"I went into the town hall," Savannah said. "And looked over all the records from around August 4th, 1893. Some of the death certificates were beyond reading, but there was enough that I was able to read."

"What does the certificates list as the cause of death?" Heidi asked.

"Unnatural causes," Savannah said flatly.

"Unnatural causes?" Heidi said. "That doesn't make any sense."

"A curse would be an unnatural cause, right?" Roxy asked. "That would mean that this place is cursed. We should get out of here as quickly as we can. Screw the dark, let's leave now."

"Calm down, Roxy," Jennifer said. "We're not going anywhere. We are staying here until we find the guys. I'm not leaving without Mike."

"We can't hike out tonight," Savannah said. "Not in the dark. There's too many trails that we could get lost on. I'm sure the police are out by this point. They will be the group that finds the guys. Maybe they found a trail that we missed. Maybe we missed each other. The guys got back, found that we had come here, and are now out looking for us. The point is, something bad happened here. I'm getting this strange feeling, something isn't right."

"You sure it isn't that time of the month?" Heidi asked.

"Positive," Savannah said. "We need to be careful. We'll have to stand watch tonight. Each person take a shift again."

"I've been here for so long and I'm fine," Melanie said. "There's nothing in the diary written about that day. There was no mention of a mass death or problems in town. I don't know what to say. I've looked over a lot of information about this town, but I've never come across anything that would indicate a curse or that there was some type of problem here."

"Okay," Savannah said. "Leah, come with me. We are going to bed now and will take the first two shifts."

"Sure," Leah said taking another drink before standing up. "We can do that."

"Someone stay up until around midnight," Savannah said, "then wake me up."

Savannah and Leah walked towards the town hall. Savannah hoped that no one was suspicious about what she said, but she was sure she played it cool. The pair got into the hall and

Leah started to walk to where the beds were, but Savannah motioned her into the records room.

"What are we doing in here?" Leah said sitting down at one of the desks.

"We're in big trouble," Savannah said. "I mean big trouble."

"What?" Leah asked.

"Most of the records list unnatural causes. I found some other papers from that time."

"What do they say?" Leah asked.

"There was a wedding," Savannah said. "An eighteen-year-old girl got married to a twenty-year-old man."

"Why's that strange"? Leah asked.

"Nothing strange about that," Savannah said. "They were both from very prominent families of the area. The entire town was invited to the wedding and after party."

"That'd be a hell of a party," Leah said. "What happened?"

"Turns out the bride had a sister," Savannah said. "A younger sister that was jealous. She wanted to get married, wanted a wedding of her own. When her parents told her no she ran into the forest and returned on August 4th, 1983. She had married a man she'd met in the forest."

"Weird," Leah said. "But that still doesn't explain what happened to everyone. I mean, there had to be something about how the people died."

"There is," Savannah said. "The newspaper said that the man was a wizard…"

"Hold on," Leah said. "Wizard? Are you kidding me? There's no such thing as a wizard."

"They may be using the wrong term," Savannah said. "Maybe something like a shaman would be better. Wizard implies old Europe, shaman would indicate a more native style magic."

"Magic?"

"If this story is true," Savannah said. "It says that the shaman had been banned from the town for using magic. He would not be welcomed into town unless someone invited him in. They claim that when he met the girl, he was in a different form—a young, strapping, handsome man. When he entered the town, however, he turned into an old man. He turned on everyone, including his new bride. He killed until the townsfolk were able to burn him. In his final death throws, he cursed the town and his bride."

"What does the curse say?" Leah asked.

"They never go into specifics," Savannah said. "But a few years later anyone who was left, and hadn't died a strange death, left the town."

"I'm not saying that I believe any of this, but do you think that the guys could have ran into the curse?" Leah asked.

"I'm betting they did," Savannah said.

"Why do you say that?" Leah asked.

"Because of this."

Savannah tossed a newspaper on the desk in front of Leah. Leah picked up the paper and looked at the picture on the front page. It was a wedding picture, a beautiful bride, handsome groom, but standing next to the bride was her sister, Sophia Melanie Larsen.

Chapter 14

Leah had never sobered up faster than she had in the moment when she looked at the newspaper. In a paper dated over one hundred years before was a picture of a girl who'd just served her dinner and moonshine. Leah studied the paper before looking back a Savannah, who had a blank expression on her face.

"What does this mean?" Leah stuttered, scared.

"It means that this town is haunted," Savannah said. "We're in deep trouble."

"What do we do?" Leah asked. "If this is real, then that means we've been talking with a dead person. This has to be a hoax, right?"

"A hoax?" Savannah asked. "Like Melanie just planted all this information with the hopes of a group of people arriving, finding, and piecing all of it together. Leah, we were talking to a dead girl. I'm sure that the guys met up with her too. Those shadows out there? I bet they're the townsfolk. They must be bound to this town somehow; maybe they aren't allowed to leave."

"How do we get out of here?" Leah asked. "Do we leave now?"

"If we followed the river," Savannah said. "We would come out near the beach. The problem is there are a lot of nocturnal animals, big cats, and other surprises that could be awake and looking for a light snack."

"We could chance swimming though," Leah said. "I mean, it's not like we're in jeans and heavy sweat shirts, most of us are wearing bikinis. We could swim the river."

"There's rapids," Savannah said. "It would be far too dangerous."

"You want to stay here until its daylight?" Leah asked.

"I really think we should," Savannah said. "It would be safer. If Melanie meant us harm, she would have hurt us by now. The fact that we're safe tells me that Melanie has other plans. We need to be careful."

"Other plans?" Leah asked. "What could she want...wait a moment, when I was talking with her Melanie talked about how lonely she was getting here. How she wanted companions and friends to be here with her."

"She may plan to bind us to the town. We'd never be able to leave," Savannah said.

"All things considered," Leah said, "the only reason I'm not a total mess right now is because of how buzzed I am."

"Your point being?"

"Why are you so calm?" Leah asked. "If I wasn't drunk, I'd be freaking out. I would be a total mess, unable to function at all. How are you holding it together?"

"Training," Savannah said. "A good military commander has to be able to hold strong and fast any time any situation arises. I've had years of practice."

"You've prepared to meet a ghost?"

"Not a ghost," Savannah said. "But intense situations. Hostile environments. Situations where it's easy to break down. Look Leah, I have no intentions of dying up here tonight. I have no intentions of being trapped up here either."

"Then what do we do?" Leah asked.

"We have no choice but to stay the night," Savannah said. "Even if I thought it were possible to navigate the river, you're too drunk and Roxy isn't strong enough. She'd never make it. We're all tired and worn out."

"So we stay the night," Leah said. "Then what? How do we get away from Melanie?"

"I need to work on that," Savannah said. "We'll have to gather information to try and find her weakness. Maybe we can do something to make sure she lets us go."

"Like what?"

"I don't know," Savannah said. "What do you know about ghosts? Are there any rumors or legends on how to get rid of them?"

"I don't know," Leah said. "I can't think right now. I don't know what we should do. Did you find any more information about her?"

"No," Savannah said. "Just that the shaman killed a lot of people that day, August 4th 1893. He killed without mercy."

"Did it say why?"

"This town was founded on the graveyard of his people," Savannah said. "That was the rumor. That's what people spoke about. They also said that no graves were ever found. No bodies were found that could have been his people. They never really talked about anything else. They said the man tricked Melanie by looking like a handsome young man, but once she invited him into the town he changed."

"This is too much," Leah said. "I must have passed out from drinking too much. I've known you a long time, Savannah. I've never once heard you talk like this. I've never heard you talk that you believe in ghosts and supernatural. Why do you believe this?"

"Look at where we are," Savannah said. "Look at everything that's happened. I know this seems incredible, but it feels real. There's something telling me that we are in the presence of something that isn't human. I can't really explain it, but I have a feeling. I know it might be strange, but I always follow my gut, my instincts. They've never led me wrong."

"And you don't think it would be better if we ran?"

"I don't," Savannah said.

"What if we called the rangers?" Leah said. "You still have the walkie-talkie. Call them with our position. Use the GPS to give them longitude and latitude. They could be here in an hour and we'd be safe."

"I really don't think Melanie would take kindly to them coming here," Savannah said. "She seems friendly enough now, but just wait until a bunch rangers or police show up. It might be a very different story."

"Really?" Leah said. "You're going to hold off on getting help because of that? We have the radio, Savannah. I'm making a call whether you like it or not."

"I didn't say we couldn't," Savannah said. "I was just telling you to think of all the things that could happen if we did."

"The radio won't work here," a female voice said from behind them.

Savannah and Leah quickly spun around, Savannah with her gun drawn, to see Brandi standing in the doorway. She looked hurt, like she'd been beat up. She was still only wearing her lifeguard suit, but her skin was dirty and there were rope burns on her wrists and ankles. Brandi grimaced in pain.

"What's going on? Who hurt you?"

"Lacey did this to me," Brandi said. "We were coming up to find you. There are police on the main trails. We figured that you were on the hidden trails. I wanted to find you, but Lacey wouldn't let me. She beat me up and tied me to a tree, hoping that an animal, or the shadows would get me. That bitch couldn't finish me off herself. Even if that radio works, Lacey and Morris wouldn't help you. They know better than to walk on the hidden trails."

"What do you mean?" Savannah asked.

"The trails are haunted," Brandi said. "Melanie is evil. She will kill all of you. I'm betting that she killed the guys. It's what she does. Every once in a while she will come down to the main trails and capture someone. She loves doing it. Melanie loves killing."

"What do we do then?" Savannah asked. "How do we get out of here?"

"We have to run," Brandi said. "The trail to the north will eventually branch in two directions. If we go west, then we will get to private land in less than a mile. There's a camp there: a group of loggers who get specialty trees down from the mountain. They have trucks that could get us out of the forest."

"Are there good trails there?" Leah asked. "You know the way or are there all kinds of branches to the trail so we may be getting lost as we go along?"

"I know the way," Brandi said. "I can get us there."

"What about the others?" Savannah asked. "How do we get them to come with us without alerting Melanie that something is wrong?"

"We'll have to leave them and come back in the morning," Brandi said.

"No," Savannah said. "How can you even ask us that? We've come this far with them. We are not leaving our friends here to die alone in the forest."

"If you don't come with me," Brandi said, "you will die with them in this forest. There's no way to prevent that. Melanie will kill you. She kills everyone that enters her lair. It's nothing more than a game to her."

"We will wait until everyone is asleep," Savannah said. "I will silently wake them up and get them to follow us. Melanie will never know that we are leaving."

"She's a ghost!" Brandi almost yelled. "You cannot sneak away as a group. Your best hope is to get to the camp and have the loggers come back here at first light."

"Can Melanie not go out in the light?" Leah asked. "Can she only function at night?"

"She was out in the light earlier," Savannah said. "What difference does it make?"

"She more powerful at night," Brandi said. "Not by much, but if we had a group of people with us during the day, she might let us leave."

"What can we do to stop her?" Savannah asked. "You've been here a long time, has anyone ever walked out of this town after they met Melanie? Are there other ghosts?"

"I've never heard of any other ghosts," Brandi said. "And I've never seen anyone walk out of here alive. We would be the first if we made it. Look, Savannah, I know you and I haven't seen eye-to-eye, maybe I was jealous of your athletic talent. Maybe I was jealous of how those guys were spending all their time trying to impress me and get my attention, but once you came around, they ignored me and were all over you. The point is, we need to work together to get out of this. Can we put the past behind us?"

"I suppose," Savannah said. "Don't thinks this makes us friends, Brandi. I'm still beyond pissed at you for how you humiliated me. But, yes, we can work together to get out of here."

"Then we need to go right now," Brandi said.

"We can't leave them though," Savannah said.

"We can't do anything to help them if we're dead," Brandi said. "If Melanie finds out that I'm trying to get you out of here, then all will be lost. She'll just kill us."

"Leah," Savannah said, "what do you think?"

"If we can't do anything for them," Leah said, "we should just go. You told them we were going to bed. There's no reason they'd be looking for us."

"They will at midnight when I told them to wake us up to stand guard," Savannah said. "If we're not here, then they'll all know that something is wrong."

"Write them a note," Brandi said. "Tell them that you two are outside the perimeter of the town, standing guard for the group."

"Wouldn't Melanie suspect something though?" Leah asked.

"She wouldn't even know," Savannah said. "It will most likely be Heidi on watch duty. Roxy and Jennifer will be sleeping. I can write a note, I know what to say so Heidi won't worry."

"Do you really think that we can do this?" Leah said. "I mean, there's a lot of animals in those woods right now. We may be safer with the ghost."

"If we don't do something," Savannah said, "we'll die here. I don't like this one bit, but if we can get out of here we should. Brandi, do you have a map that we can look at?"

"Where would I carry a map wearing this?" Brandi asked.

"There's a map in the room over here," Leah said.

The Savannah and Brandi went into the records room as Leah took a map out of a drawer and set it on one of the desks. They spread the map open and smoothed it out. Savannah took a flashlight out of her pack and shined it over the map. Brandi began pointing at different points on the map.

"We are here," Brandi said.

"There's nothing on the map there," Savannah said. "Why isn't this town on any maps?"

"Once the evil took this town no one wanted anything to do with it," Brandi said looking over the map, tracing a trail with her finger. "This is where the logging camp is. As I said, it's under two miles but it will be very difficult hiking, the trails haven't been kept up and they are very rugged. We won't be able to move very fast on them."

"That's fine," Savannah said as she took some paper, a pen, and began to write her note. "As long as we can make it to the logger's camp, we'll be able to save the others."

"Then let's go," Leah said.

Savannah finished the note, walked over to her bed, and placed it on the covers. Savannah checked her gun and then led Brandi and Leah out of the town hall and towards the trees. The girls were careful not to be noticed by the others sitting by the fire. Savannah looked at Melanie, amazed that she was looking at a ghost. The girls had just entered the trail on the trees when Savannah stopped and confronted Brandi.

"Hang on one second," Savannah said in a hushed tone. "How do we know that you're not messing with us? How do I know that you aren't still trying to humiliate me for what happened so long ago? You show up here, feed us that story, and for some reason, we are just supposed to trust you?"

"Savannah," Brandi said. "If I lied to you, you can do whatever you want to me—beat me up, plot out some elaborate way to humiliate me. If I lied to you, you can do anything to me. Leah is the witness to me telling you this, okay?"

"Okay," Savannah said thinking it over. "Let's move out."

Chapter 15

Heidi jolted awake. She'd been having a dream that she was falling and when she hit the ground, she woke up. Her eyes were barely open, but she could feel that her body was covered in a sweat from the hot night air as well. Heidi's mouth was dry and she felt sluggish and thirsty.

She started to sit up before she fully opened her eyes. She was very tired when the others had gone to bed and left her to take the first watch. Heidi still felt tired, like she hadn't slept very long. She knew that since she could remember the dream that she hadn't been sleeping soundly.

Heidi opened her eyes and her heart almost stopped. It was light out. Heidi was supposed to wake Savannah up at midnight to take over the watch but here she'd slept until it was light out. It took Heidi more than a second to realize that it being light outside wasn't the reason her heart had almost stopped. Heidi fully opened her eyes and realized that somehow, someway, Amber Hollow was now bright, vibrant, and alive.

The streets of Amber Hollow were full of people going about in a hurried hustle and bustle. There were people going about their day on this sultry, humid morning. Heidi slowly stood up and looked around. The town looked new, every building had activity in and around it. Everyone was dressed in summer clothing that appeared to be from around 1890. Heidi's brain tried to explain what was going on, but she couldn't figure it out.

Heidi slowly started to walk down the street. She needed to make way for horses and carriages that were moving swiftly down the roads. Once Heidi started moving around, many people started to notice her. As she passed a woman, she heard her say, "Whore,"

Heidi looked down, realizing what she was wearing; a red bikini top covered with yellow splashes with matching board shorts and figured that the people here hadn't seen any clothing like it before. It dawned on Heidi that many people might be staring at her because she was black.

Heidi couldn't figure out which way she should walk first until she saw the town hall. It looked amazing in the morning sun. She thought that some of the other girls should be around here and the hall would be the first place they would go. Heidi started to run into the hall as more people began commenting on her and her clothing. She heard people saying everything from tart to witch to tramp. She also heard some people hurling racial slurs towards her.

Heidi started to race to the town hall. She'd always loved wearing clothing that accented her sexy body and had never once cared if a person glared at her or whispered a name behind her back but here Heidi felt exposed. She didn't care for the hurtful things they were saying. She couldn't figure out which comments were worse, the remarks about her skin or her clothing. As she was about to go up the stairs to the town hall, the sheriff, a tall, thin, rough-looking man with a Stetson hat and handlebar mustache stepped in her way stopping Heidi in her tracks. Heidi instantly recognized him as the man that gave the girls the warning in the park.

"Sorry, ma'am," the sheriff said. "I don't know what you think you're doing, but 'round here, in these parts, we have decency laws. There's no decorum in the outfit you're wearing."

"Sheriff," Heidi said, quickly thinking up a lie. "Something happened to me. A feller took my clothing and he wouldn't give them back. I had to run out of the forest with nothing but this on. He ripped my dress right off of me."

"That's a high crime there, young lady," the sheriff said. "Man could get himself in a whole heap of trouble for taking advantage of a young lass. You know who he was?"

"I don't," Heidi said. "I'd never seen him before. He attacked me."

"You'd best get inside," the sheriff said. "We don't need to corrupt more people or any children by letting them see you like that."

The sheriff escorted Heidi into the building. Inside the heat was unbearable. Heidi couldn't figure out how all of the people could be in the building with heavy dresses, long sleeves, and layers when it was this hot. Even in what she was wearing Heidi, was still hot and sweating. As she was walking through the building, the stench was almost excruciating. None of the sweating people had ever heard of deodorant and they only took baths once a month. Heidi could figure which was worse, the smell of sweat or the horse shit.

The sheriff took Heidi into a back room and motioned her to sit down at a table. Heidi quickly sat down, looking around for any sign of her friends. When they'd gone to bed, every one of the girls had their stomachs exposed with a bikini or athletic top and they were all wearing short shorts. Every one of them would have been treated the same as Heidi was. Heidi was confident that none of the others had been through this, otherwise the sheriff would have made mention of it.

"You're not from here," the sheriff said. "What brings you to these parts?"

"Just traveling through," Heidi said

The sheriff chewed at his lower lip while he stared at Heidi, right at her bikini top, not even bothering to hide what he was staring at. Heidi hoped that she wouldn't have to create an entire backstory for this guy. She knew that she could do things to him that no girl or woman in this time even knew about. She wondered if she could get him out of his clothes so she could get out of here. Her mind was still swimming with the fact that she had travelled through time.

"Interesting choice of clothing," the sheriff said as he reached out and felt the strap of Heidi's top. "I've never seen nor felt a fabric like this before. What is it?"

"Spandex," Heidi said quickly. "It's called a bikini. It's made for swimming but I wear tops like this when I'm out hiking in the woods with my friends. They're more comfortable and works great when you're really hot."

"I must say," the sheriff said, "I've never seen woman look as stunning as you. I think your bikini makes you look stunning. I mean, you're an amazing looking woman to begin with but that top, I do declare, makes you look like an angel. Where could I get one for my wife?"

"I doubt a store around here carries them," Heidi said. "They're very rare."

"Interesting." The sheriff felt the strap a little more before moving his hand to the side of the top. He was applying a good amount of pressure as he rubbed the side of Heidi's breast. She wanted to push his hand away, wanted to slap him for what he was doing, but on the other hand, he was a powerful, handsome man. She didn't want to upset anyone, especially the sheriff. Heidi just wanted to find her friends and figure out what was going on here. As Heidi was trying to figure out what she should do the sheriff's hand went to the front of her breast as the sheriff licked his lips as Heidi looked into his predatory eyes. Heidi quickly, but firmly reached up and pulled his hand away.

"Easy there, Sheriff," Heidi said slyly. "I know you like this material, but I doubt that your wife would like you feeling it there."

"My wife wouldn't like me doing that much at all," the sheriff said. "But it seems like you didn't have a problem with me doing it."

"Maybe I didn't," Heidi said. "Maybe I did. I have a lot of questions, Sheriff. I have to find some of my friends and figure out what's going on here. Are you going to send out a deputy to arrest the man that tried to take advantage of me?"

"I would send a man out if I believed your story," the sheriff said. "Here's the problem that I have: I was warned about a woman like you hanging 'round these parts, trying to drum up some business, if you catch my drift."

"It wasn't me," Heidi said.

"Not many other colored women in these parts that walk around without many clothes on," the sheriff said. "You fit the description perfectly."

"Is there another officer here?" Heidi asked. "A deputy who can watch what goes on here. I don't trust you anymore."

"Hey!" the sheriff shouted. "Get in here right now!" Heidi smiled knowing that with someone else in the room the sheriff wouldn't be able to take advantage of her. Heidi didn't know what he was going to do but she wanted a witness. Heidi's elation didn't last long when Melanie appeared with a black Stetson hat along with a deputy's badge pinned to the strap of her top. Melanie smiled as she walked into the room and looked Heidi over.

"Well, aren't you the cat's meow?" Melanie asked with a twisted smile. "You think that you could saunter into Amber Hollow and go to work," Melanie snapped her fingers, "just like that? You really think that we would let you do that?"

"A female deputy?" Heidi asked trying to wrap her head around this. "I didn't know women could even hold jobs now."

"I take what I want, Heidi," Melanie said.

"How the hell did you know my name?" Heidi asked. "I haven't said it yet since I've been in this town."

"I've spoken with you before," Melanie said. "Just like I talked with Savannah, Leah, Roxy, and Jennifer. Just like I spoke with Mike, Todd, Greg, and Steve."

"You bitch," Heidi said jumping up and advancing. "Let's go right now." Heidi tried to walk up to Melanie but the sheriff stepped in her way. Heidi tried to get around him but he powerfully held her where she was. Heidi couldn't understand any of this. She tried to struggle with the sheriff but she knew that he could overpower her any time he wanted.

"Just calm down Heidi," Melanie said. "You have nothing to fear."

"What is going on here?" Heidi asked. "Where are all my friends?"

"Roxy and Jennifer are sleeping in the town hall where you left them," Melanie said. "Savannah and Leah have left the town with another girl, Brandi, that little worker from the park. They are attempting to get to a logging camp where they believe that men there will help."

"No way," Heidi said. "No way would Savannah go with Brandi. Those two hate each other. Savannah wouldn't go with her and she wouldn't leave all of us."

"She did though," Melanie said. "Everyone is where I say they are."

"Then take me to Jennifer," Heidi said. "Take me to her now."

"That I can't do," Melanie said.

"Why not?"

"Because they are where you left them," Melanie said. "Right in the town hall."

"That's where we are at, right?" Heidi asked.

"We may be in the same place," Melanie said. "But this is a different time, my time."

"But you're so young," Heidi said. "You were never the deputy of Amber Hollow. What are you doing?"

"When I became this way," Melanie said. "I found I could control things in many different ways. I found I could do things. I love destroying people. I have some fun things planned for the rest of your friends. They will suffer before I destroy them. Here's the greatest part, I've got a few other people here that they will love to meet. Please welcome the rest of the police force. Come on in, guys!"

From a side door, Mike, Todd, Greg, and Steve rushed in the room. They were all in deputies clothing from the 1890's. They all had badges. None of them seemed to recognize Heidi for who she was, a friend of theirs. They were all ogling her in her bikini top. Heidi wished she could have covered up. She didn't like the way they were staring at her.

"Mike," Heidi said. "Jennifer will be so happy to see you. You cannot believe how worried she's been about you. She brought us out to the forest to search for you, the whole time claiming that she wouldn't leave without you."

"He doesn't know what you're talking about," Melanie said. "He's already died, just like you will very quickly." Heidi's heart skipped a beat. At first she thought that she misheard Melanie, but with the way the men were staring at her, she knew that she heard her correctly. Heidi had to think quickly if she wanted to get out of this one.

"What do you want?" Heidi asked. "I'll do anything to get my friends back."

"I have everything," Melanie said. "All I want is to watch people suffer. Seize her!"

The four guys rushed around Heidi and grabbed her. Heidi tried to fight them but she wasn't strong enough to take on any one of them, let alone all four at the same time. They quickly held Heidi off the ground.

"I want you to struggle," Melanie said. "I want you to beg for your life. I want you to curse me as I torment you. I want you to fight this."

"Go to hell," Heidi said as she spit in Melanie's face. "Go to hell and stay there, bitch."

"To the gallows with her," Melanie commanded.

The guys quickly carried Heidi outside the town hall. Everyone started watching as the guys made all kinds of noise about what they were doing. The crowd watched and started making nasty comments about Heidi. She knew that death was not far off.

In the town square was a gallows, a massive wooden platform raised about the square with a tall post that had a noose hanging from it. The men quickly carried Heidi up to the platform and got her into position, putting the noose around her neck. The crowd was growing, almost everyone stopped to watch. The crowd cheered. Heidi took a deep breath as she noticed Melanie walking up. Melanie wasted no time in throwing the switch. In an instant, Heidi felt like she was falling, the ground had given out beneath her. Before she could realize what had happened, the rope snapped, and Heidi's limp body was slightly rocking in the breeze.

Chapter 16

The songs of the birds gently woke Roxy. She stretched. The bed she was sleeping on wasn't the most comfortable, but it was better than the ground. She listened to the birds sing and the bugs chirp before slowly opening her eyes.

Roxy couldn't believe what she saw. The jail looked brand new. Everything there was shiny and clean. She quickly sat up and looked around. There was no one else inside. Every other cell was empty. When she'd gone to sleep Jennifer was in the bed opposite her and Melanie was in the cell next to theirs.

Roxy got off the bed and moved around, pinching herself to make sure that she wasn't dreaming. She tried to open the cell door, but it was locked. She pushed with everything she had, but it didn't budge. She looked around for another way out, but there wasn't one. Roxy didn't see the keys anywhere either.

"Hello?" Roxy called out. "Can anyone hear me?" There was no reply. Roxy strained to listen. There were no voices, footsteps, or human sounds of any kind. She didn't know what to do. She couldn't see a way out of the cell and there was no one there to help her. There were only the two beds in the cell, nothing else. Roxy figured it must have been a temporary holding cell.

As Roxy tried to figure out what she should do, she realized just how badly she needed to go to the bathroom. There wasn't anything in the cell that she could use, not even a bucket. Roxy also realized how hot and thirsty that she was. Roxy knew that if she didn't get out of the cell soon things would get very miserable.

"Help me!" Roxy shouted at the top of her lungs. "Somebody please help me!"

This time Roxy heard footsteps. They were light and moving slowly, whoever they belonged to was being careful not to make too much noise and wasn't walking very fast, but Roxy could hear them coming her way. It took almost a minute from when she'd yelled, but finally Heidi came around the corner.

"Heidi," Roxy said breathing a sigh of relief. "Boy, am I glad to see you. What the hell is going on around here?"

"I don't know," Heidi said confusedly. "What are you doing in there?"

"I woke up like this," Roxy said. "Where were you at?"

"I was over there," Heidi pointed down a hallway. "I was sitting at a desk when you called. I don't know what I was doing before that. Things seemed to get really strange. I need to ask you a question, but this is going to sound really weird."

"What's that?"

"Does my neck look okay?"

"Your neck?"

"Yeah, my neck," Heidi said raising her head up as she walked up to the cell door. "It really hurts right now and it feels really weird."

"Interesting," Roxy said looking at Heidi. "You've got a rope burn, I think. I don't know what else could do something like that. It looks like there's some bruising."

"It feels like there's something almost trying to strangle me right now. It's really weird."

"I can help you figure it out," Roxy said, "but I need to be out of this cell. Find the keys and open the door, please."

"Okay," Heidi said. "Where do you think the keys will be at?"

"I don't know," Roxy said. "Is there a drawer or a cabinet that has a bunch of keys in it?"

"I'll check the desks," Heidi said as she disappeared down the hallway.

Roxy paced in the cell. She was scared and hoping that something would provide an answer sooner rather than later. It only took a minute before Heidi returned with a ring of keys. She quickly started trying them and at the third one, the door unlocked. Roxy rushed out and hugged her friend.

"Thank you so much," Roxy said. "I couldn't stand it in there. Who would have locked me in there? Was someone playing a trick on me or what?"

"I don't know," Heidi said. "The big problem is that the others aren't here."

"What do you mean?" Roxy asked.

"I haven't seen Savannah, Leah, Jennifer, or Melanie," Heidi said. "Neither Jennifer nor Melanie are where they went to bed last night. I don't remember what happened to me. I was on watch duty, I sat down, maybe drifted to sleep a little? I don't know. Then I woke up out there when I heard you calling. I don't remember walking in here."

"Let's go outside and retrace your steps. Maybe something will come back to you."

"There's something else I should mention, Roxy," Heidi said. "I'm not really sure how to tell you this. You notice anything strange about this cell? Notice anything strange about this room?"

"It's all fixed up and nice looking," Roxy said. "I don't get that. It wasn't like that when I went to bed last night. I don't understand it."

"Be prepared to not understand a lot, Roxy," Heidi said. "It gets weirder out there."

Roxy followed Heidi with a confused look on her face as Heidi led the way into the main offices of the town hall. Roxy wasn't prepared for what she saw. Everything in the hall had been restored overnight. It looked amazing. The rooms were freshly painted. The glass was clean and solid. The floors didn't squeak or creak. Roxy couldn't believe what she was seeing.

"How is this possible?" Roxy asked. "Is someone playing a trick on us or something?"

"I thought that at first," Heidi said. "But there is no way to do this much in such a short amount of time without waking us up. I'm sure you would have heard the work going on here and depending what time I got in here I'm sure I would have heard something as well."

"But if it's not a trick," Roxy asked. "Then what is it?"

"I don't know," Heidi said.

"What should we do?" Roxy asked.

"We need to find the others," Heidi said. "We need to get the group together and whatever we do, we need to stick together at this point. We cannot risk splitting up any more."

"Agreed," Roxy said.

The girls rushed through the town hall and out the main doors. They were stunned by what they saw. The entire town was fixed up, looking new. Roxy turned back and looked over the town hall, which would look proud standing on any city street. The streets were clean and nice and around every building was perfectly manicured landscaping.

Roxy and Heidi rushed to where they'd had their fire the night before. The area was a little park now, with benches and a small play area for children. There was a fire pit but it looked to be new, unused. There was no sign of the logs they'd been sitting on the night before. Nothing looked the same.

"This isn't right," Heidi said. "Where are we supposed to go? Where is everyone?"

"How did everything get fixed up?" Roxy asked. "There's no way Melanie could have done all of this. Where did she go?"

"Right here," Melanie's voice rang out behind them.

The girls turned and were surprised again. Melanie was coming up towards them, but she was wearing the exact same outfit that Savannah had been wearing the night before. Melanie looked like she'd had a very good night's sleep and was ready for another day. She was full of energy with a bright glow about her smile and eyes. Roxy and Heidi could only stare as she rushed up to them.

"What's going on?" Melanie asked. "Where have you two been at?"

"We were in the town hall," Roxy said. "Where were you? Where is everyone else? What happened to your clothes? How did you get into Savannah's outfit?"

"What do you mean?" Melanie asked.

"Look at what you're wearing," Roxy said. "That's what Savannah was wearing."

"You think I stole her outfit?" Melanie asked.

"No," Roxy said. "If that was Savannah's clothing you'd be drowning in it. She was much bigger than you, but yet, the clothing is exactly what she was wearing before. How?"

"I don't know," Melanie said looking over her clothing. "I just woke up like this. I was in a house over there. I don't know how I got there. What's going on with the town? How did everything get restored?"

"No idea," Roxy said. "Something strange is going on."

"I can't explain it, but something is tightening around my neck," Heidi said with concern in her voice. "It's like I can feel a rope or something."

"That's really strange," Roxy said. "There must be something to explain it."

"We need to figure out what happened to my town first," Melanie said.

"What do you suggest that we do?" Roxy said. "What are we to do? Is there somewhere we could go for answers? Is there someone in the area that could explain this?"

"There could be," Melanie said. "There's one man around here."

"One man?" Heidi asked. "Why didn't you mention him before?"

"It wasn't necessary," Melanie said. "He really doesn't like people visiting him. He keeps to himself mostly. We don't want to upset him; he has a bad temper."

"Where does he live?" Roxy asked.

"Not far from here," Melanie said. "We can walk there easy enough."

"I don't know," Roxy said. "We should look around here and see if we could find the others first. They must be around here somewhere. We can't leave without them."

"We have to do something," Heidi said. "We can't sit around and wait."

"We should search them out," Roxy said. "Let's check the town for them and see if we can find them. If we can't then we should go to that man."

"We were in the town hall," Heidi said, "and no one was in there. What building should we try next?"

"Let's go to the church," Roxy said. "That's as good a place as any to start."

Roxy took off running with Heidi and Melanie one step behind her. They rushed through the empty streets and right to the church building. The church was gorgeous. The stone foundation seemed to glimmer. The building was tall and impressive with ornate landscaping and stunning frescos paintings hung on the walls of the entry.

The girls entered the building and walked into the sanctuary. Roxy was stunned at all the wooden pews, each one with intricate carvings on the backs. Everything inside was spotlessly clean. Roxy couldn't imagine how much work it would take to keep this church in that condition. As the girls walked around the sanctuary, a priest entered the room.

The girls froze when they saw him. His expression matched theirs, seeing three strange women in his church wearing clothing that was not suitable for a church. Roxy studied the man, he was tall and lanky, in a black suit with black hair and a handlebar mustache. He walked slowly, but didn't say a word. He simply gazed at the girls. Roxy realized that he was the man who'd given them the warning in the park.

Heidi looked over the priest and couldn't help but notice that she seemed to know him from somewhere. Heidi knew that she had seen this man before, but simply couldn't place him no matter how hard she tried. The feeling that he'd hurt her kept getting stronger and stronger, however. Heidi knew that he was not someone to be trusted.

"What are you doing here?" the priest asked.

"We are looking for our friends," Roxy said. "Have you seen other women our age around here?"

"I have not," the priest said. "What are you doing, wearing clothing like that? Have you no decency?"

"What?" Roxy asked looking at her outfit. "This is what everyone wears when they go hiking. It's what we all wear. What are you talking about?"

"You need to repent, my child," the priest said. "Save your soul. It's the only way. We should pray together."

"We don't need to pray right now," Roxy said. "We need to find our friends. Please, can you help us find them? Is there anyone else around here?"

"Others around here?" the priest asked with a strange look on his face. "The town is bustling with people. There are people everywhere out there."

"What?" Roxy asked.

Roxy looked out the window of the church and realized that the priest wasn't joking. There were people everywhere. Roxy and Heidi rushed out of the church. They were stunned with what they saw. There were people hurriedly going about their day. They were all dress in attire from the 1890's and they all looked in desperate need of a shower.

As the people moved around, the priest walked up behind the women, who were both stunned silent. Roxy noticed that many of the people were starting to notice them and were making comments about their outfits. Roxy couldn't believe what was going on. She didn't know how to react. All Roxy wanted to do was find her friends and get out of there.

"Father," a man from the crowd shouted, "what are you doing with those whores?"

"Saving them," the priest said back.

"How?" the man asked.

"Build a pyre," the priest said. "We need to take care of the witches."

Roxy's eyes widened in shock as the people in the town started cheering and cat-calling. In an instant, they were collecting firewood and placing it in a pile around a large pole that had an elevated platform attached to it. Roxy swallowed in a throat that was suddenly dry. She turned to look, but Heidi was no longer there.

"What happened to Heidi?" Roxy asked.

"Who?" the priest asked.

"The other woman that was with us," Roxy said.

"You were alone," the priest said. "It was only you and Sister Melanie."

"Sister Melanie?" Roxy asked.

Roxy looked at saw that Melanie was wearing a proper nun's habit. Roxy knew that Melanie was wearing something different a moment before and knew that Heidi was with her. As Roxy tried to figure all of this out, she saw Mike, Todd, Greg, and Steve running up to her. They were all in deputy's uniforms from the period. Before Roxy could say a word, they grabbed her and carried her to the pyre.

"Stop!" Roxy shouted. "What are you doing?"

No one responded to her. None of the guys seemed to know who she was. They were silent as they took her and tied her to the pole. Roxy looked at Melanie who'd once again changed clothes, back in her original black outfit. Melanie smiled sadistically.

"Who are you?" Roxy shouted at Melanie.

"I am who I said I am," Melanie shouted back. "Melanie. This is my town and I will rule it the way I choose to."

As Roxy tried to process what Melanie said, the priest lit the pyre. The flames quickly caught and Roxy could feel the heat. The townsfolk cheered and yelled happily. Roxy struggled to find a way down. She screamed; the heat too intense. She looked to her left, and saw a hang man's noose with Heidi's lifeless body gently swaying in the breeze. It was the last thing Roxy saw before the fire engulfed her.

Chapter 17

Jennifer slowly opened her eyes. She'd been awake for a few minutes, but had kept her eyes closed due to the strange voices that she'd been hearing. She couldn't tell who they were or where they were coming from, but there were voices speaking in hushed tones. The voices seemed menacing, a growly voice with evil intentions, but Jennifer didn't hear any actual words. Jennifer debated whether the voice had been real.

Jennifer looked around the jail cell. Roxy was in one bed, Heidi in another. She noticed that Melanie wasn't in the bed that she had gone to sleep in. Jennifer noticed that Roxy appeared to be hot, almost red hot. She was pouring sweat even though she had no covers on top of her and was only wearing a bikini top and board shorts. Jennifer noted that Heidi's hands were around her neck, like she was scratching an itch or something.

Jennifer wondered what time it was. It was still dark out and she knew that she hadn't been asleep for very long. She figured they'd gone to bed around midnight, Jennifer wanted to stay up late in the hopes that the guys would come wandering through. Jennifer wondered what Mike was up to right now. She wondered what kind of stories that the guys would have for them. Jennifer imagined that when they got back, they would go to the bar, order burgers and beer, and laugh the night away at how silly the girls were in thinking that they needed to go rescue them.

As Jennifer's mind was on the future, a noise in the present drew her attention. There were footsteps within the town hall. She couldn't tell where the steps were coming from, but she could tell that they were above her, from the second floor. The girls had searched a lot of area within the town, but hadn't yet ventured upstairs. Jennifer thought it strange, so she lit a candle and started looking for the stairs. She searched all over the main floor to find a staircase and found it odd that it was hidden in a side room. Jennifer looked around before making her way up.

Every step creaked as she ascended. There were shadows being cast around. Jennifer knew there was a bright full moon out tonight and she figured the top platform of the stairs must be near a window. Jennifer got to the top of the platform and was stunned by what she saw, it was a storage room with filing cabinets covering ever wall and even more in the middle of the room. It looked like the second floor of the town hall was nothing but filing cabinets.

Jennifer stared in wonder. She couldn't figure out how there could be so many files in this little town. Jennifer walked to the nearest file and opened it up, pulling out the papers inside. The files appeared to be very detailed records of the area. What crops were planted each year, who had which cattle, how many trees were harvested and shipped down the river. The amount of detail was impressive. Jennifer couldn't figure out why this would be here, but then she heard the footsteps again.

Jennifer looked up and around. She didn't see anyone in the room, but she did see a shadow move along the wall. It looked like it was human. Jennifer wanted to call out, but didn't know if that would be a good idea. She realized that whoever was up there with her most likely knew she was there as well so she didn't see the harm in announcing herself.

"Hello?" Jennifer called out. "Who's there?"

At first, there was no reply but then Jennifer heard the footsteps again. They sounded like they were coming towards her. Jennifer looked around but she didn't see Melanie until she was almost on top of her. Jennifer jumped when she saw her.

"Melanie," Jennifer said breathing a sigh of relief. "Thank God. I thought I heard footsteps up here and wanted to see what was going on."

"I'm just going through some records," Melanie said. "I scan these to help me plan the best way to bring back this town. I hope I can find some ways to make it grow better than it did."

"That's a good plan," Jennifer said. "Do these records tell you anything?"

"They tell me lots," Melanie said. "The amount of information here is priceless. Not only economically, but for its historical value as well. I find the past so interesting, don't you?"

"Sometimes," Jennifer said. "But there are other times when I wish the past would just stay in the past."

"Why is that?"

"Because."

"Does it have anything to do with Mike?" Melanie asked. "Did you hurt him?"

"That's an odd question," Jennifer said. "And kind of rude, considering we barely know each other."

"You don't seem like the type who's ready to be married," Melanie said. "You seem so young. All your friends want to stay young, but here you are, being all grown up and getting married. Is there more behind it than love?"

"I'm not pregnant," Jennifer said flatly, "if that's what you are trying to get at."

"I didn't suggest that," Melanie said. "I just wonder if there's more to your marriage than you let on. How did you and Mike meet?"

"We met in college," Jennifer said. "Freshman year. We had a couple classes together, had to work as partners in one of the classes, then one night we were both at the same party. He asked me to dance. I said yes. End of story."

"Has it been smooth sailing ever since?" Melanie asked. "Or have there been some bumps along the way?"

"There have been some bumps," Jennifer said. "But what relationship is perfect?"

"What happened?"

"I'm not telling you about my relationship," Jennifer said. "I barely know you."

"You didn't come out here to find Mike, did you?" Melanie asked. "You came out to confirm that the relationship was a sham. When the rangers said that there were missing girls, you knew what happened didn't you? Did anyone tell you what they found in the tents?"

"Leah did, yes," Jennifer said. "But two tops don't prove a thing, plus they weren't in Mike's tent. The other guys were with them. Mike would never cheat on me."

"But you've cheated on him," Melanie said.

"No, I haven't," Jennifer almost shouted. "Wait a minute, how did you know about the rangers calling us? Or what we found in the tents? How do you know about that?"

"I have my ways," Melanie said.

"What happened to the tents?" Jennifer asked. "Where did they go? Did the guys pack up and leave and we just missed their note?"

"I don't think you're being very truthful," Melanie said. "Did you ever cheat on Mike?"

"I'm not answering you."

"Answer truthfully and I will tell you everything."

"I told you no!"

"And that's a lie," Melanie shouted. "You know it's a lie."

"Okay," Jennifer said. "I cheated on him, many times. The first two years of the relationship, I was with other guys more than I was with him. I wanted to be a party girl. I didn't want to be in a relationship. But, I loved Mike so much that I didn't want to lose him either. I know it was a bad thing to do, but it happened."

"You still cheat on him?" Melanie asked. "You still sleep with other men even though you're going to say your vows in a week?"

"I don't," Jennifer said. "I haven't been with anyone else since sophomore year."

"You bitch," Mike's voice rang out from behind her.

Jennifer spun around to see Mike standing at the top of the stairs. Somehow, he'd gotten to the top without her hearing him. Jennifer couldn't believe that he was standing there, alive and well, her heart was skipping for joy, yet she realized what he'd probably just heard. Jennifer didn't care. She rushed over to him and hugged him, squeezing him as tightly as she could.

"I love you, Mike," Jennifer said kissing him all over. "I love you so much. All I could think about was finding you. We came out here as quickly as we could. I'm so happy you're okay."

"But there were other guys," Mike said not reciprocating any of the affection. "The other guys that you lied about, snuck around with? What? I'm just supposed to forget about that?"

"It's not like that, Mike," Jennifer said pleadingly. "It was so long ago and they were all meaningless. It was just sex, nothing more. There was never an emotional connection like we have. I've given you my heart completely...wait a second, you knew about them."

"While you gave them everything else," Mike said. "How can I trust you Jennifer?"

"I was young and stupid," Jennifer said. "We've been through this before Mike. I thought we were past this. I was young and stupid and it's over."

"No, you're not," Mike said. "You're not stupid. You knew just what you were doing."

"Please Mike," Jennifer begged, "I love you more than anything else. What can I do to make it up to you? Anything you want, ask anything of me."

"I've always been faithful to you," Mike said. "Would you let me sleep with another?"

Jennifer was appalled by the thought of the question. Letting someone else have Mike was the last thing she wanted to do. She couldn't figure out why he was acting like this. He wasn't a saint and there was times that he'd messed up, never that bad, but he did. What she couldn't figure out was why he would ask for that. If he loved her, he should be faithful to her. Jennifer just wanted to go home and have things the way they were before.

"Who would you sleep with?" Jennifer asked hoping that he wouldn't have an answer.

"Melanie," Mike said.

"What?" Jennifer asked stunned. "She's so young. That's disgusting."

"Emotionally and maturity wise," Mike said, "She's older than you. She's lived here on her own and is developing this city to be something. That's more than you have ever done."

"Wait a second," Jennifer said trying to focus on one thing at a time. "How do you know what Melanie has done for this town? Melanie said that she didn't see you guys."

"I like to lie," Melanie said. "It's my pastime, messing with people who wander into my town. I knew exactly how to get Mike up here when I wanted him. I've heard you talk in the past, on past camping trips, I listen. I knew what you'd done. I love messing with people."

"You bitch," Jennifer said taking a step towards her. "I should mess you up right now."

"You could try," Melanie said. "But you wouldn't get anywhere. You cannot beat me."

"And I suppose that you would take Mike?" Jennifer said. "If I said yes to this, you would take him?"

"He's stunningly handsome," Melanie said. "I bet it would be fun. As I've said, I get so lonely up here. I want more friends. I want more people. Maybe I should marry him. He'd make a great husband for me."

"He's mine," Jennifer said stepping closer. "You can sleep with him over my dead body."

"Such an interesting expression," Melanie said. "I think that could be arranged."

Jennifer paused, confused, but before she had time to fully process it, Melanie and Mike disappeared from the room. Jennifer rubbed her eyes, but there was only a mist hanging in the air. She couldn't figure out what she'd just seen. There was a mocking laugh in the air. Jennifer looked around, but there was nothing there.

She hurried down the stairs and back to the jail. She stopped dead in her tracks when she realized that both Roxy and Heidi were gone. There was no indication as to where they could have gone or what had happened to them. Jennifer was worried when she heard a noise that she was very familiar with. Somewhere, two people were having sex. Jennifer could hear the moans of a woman in ecstasy. Jennifer prayed that it wasn't who she thought it was.

Jennifer raced through the town hall, getting closer to the sounds. As she peaked in the room where the noises were coming from she saw what she didn't want to see. Mike and Melanie were spread out on a blanket on the floor having a naughty, fun time. Jennifer rushed out of the building, tears welling in her eyes. She couldn't believe that he would do that to her. Jennifer wanted to kill him, but she tried to see things from his point of view. Discovering that she hadn't been faithful to him must have been very difficult.

As Jennifer tried to rationalize what Mike was doing, a thought crossed her mind: where were the other guys? Why didn't Mike tell her what had happened to them? Mike appeared out of nowhere then disappeared in a flash as well. Jennifer looked around the town, which was lit up by a bright, almost full moon. The town looked scary. There was something there, something that Jennifer couldn't figure out.

As Jennifer strained to see in the darkness, she realized that there were shadows moving around the town. The shadows were the size of people, but Jennifer couldn't make any of them out. They seemed to move quickly, darting back and forth, not staying still for a second. Jennifer had never seen anything like them before. She didn't know what was going on when she heard screaming coming from the center of town.

Jennifer rushed toward the sound only to see a flaming pyre with Roxy being burned alive. Next to her, Heidi's lifeless body swung in the breeze from a noose. Jennifer dropped to her knees and started to cry. There was nothing that she could do for either of them. Jennifer didn't know what she should do. This all felt like a dream to her. She tried pinching herself to wake herself up, but it wasn't a dream. It was real and people were dying.

"There was no way to avoid this," Mike said from behind her.

Jennifer turned to see Mike walking up to her. He was alone, but looked to be sweaty and glowing. A gleam in his eye let Jennifer know that he'd just had a very good time. Mike walked up to Jennifer and stopped, looking at the burning pile.

"So sad," Mike said. "I always thought that she would go far, once she broke out of her shell and grew up a little."

"How can you say that?" Jennifer yelled at him. "Our friends are dying and you just slept with a teenager. What happened to you guys? Why didn't you answer the phone? Why did you call me and warn me?"

"I was forced to call you," Mike said. "Melanie forced me to."

"That little girl?" Jennifer asked. "You expect me to believe that she forced you to do anything? Her and what army?"

"That little girl is a ghost," Mike said flatly. "It was kind of hard to resist then."

"Are you dead?" Jennifer asked.

"Yes."

"How are you here then?" Jennifer asked. "Why did you do this to us?"

"Melanie," Mike said. "She wants people to live in her town. We all live here now, along with all the people who died on August 4th, 1893. Her husband was vicious when he entered the town.

He forced Melanie to watch as everyone died. Then, he killed her. That's why this was abandoned. They know that Melanie is still here."

"Why was he banned from the town?" Jennifer asked.

"He was a trickster," Mike said. "He could take other forms, he could kill in strange ways. He wanted revenge and Melanie wanted a husband."

"What do we do now though?" Jennifer asked. "I love you Mike. I want to be with you. I cannot be apart from you."

"There's only one way," Mike said. "You must be dead to stay here."

"Is there any way to save you?"

"No."

"So I need to die?" Jennifer asked. "How?"

"Doesn't matter," Mike said. "You just need to die. If you don't do it, Melanie will kill you. She will go out of her way to make it painful and cruel."

"I understand," Jennifer said. Jennifer walked back into the town hall and to the records room. She'd seen a letter opener that looked sharp. She found the opener and held it in her hand. She looked back to Mike who smiled. Jennifer handed the opener to him.

"I can't do it," Jennifer said putting her hands on her head. "Stab me in the heart."

"I can't," Mike said.

"You have to," Jennifer said. "I can't kill myself."

Mike nodded, took a deep breath, and stabbed Jennifer in the heart multiple times. As Jennifer's body fell to the ground, she appeared beside Mike. The pair kissed and walked out of the hall.

Chapter 18

Savannah, Leah, and Brandi ran through the forest, hoping that they were close to the logging camp. Savannah tried to keep track of their pace, years of running had trained her on how to gauge distances. She knew that they'd been running for about a mile and a half. Leah was lagging behind them, but neither Brandi nor Savannah were slowing down. Savannah started to gain respect for Brandi. She was impressed that she was able to keep up with her.

Leah was so far behind that they would lose sight of her around the curves. The women slowed as they entered the logging camp. It was quiet. The camp was an organized mess of heavy equipment with the road lined with big, yellow, tracked equipment. The girls stopped and looked over the site. There were two long, temporary housing units on the north side of the camp and an office trailer next to them.

Savannah looked closer at the camp. Something caught her eye and didn't seem right. Savannah looked closer at some of the equipment and that's when she realized what the issue was;

the license tags on all the trucks were three years out of date. Savannah could understand one or two vehicles being out of date, but as she quickly rushed through all the trucks, they were all three years expired.

"What is it, Savannah?" Leah asked.

"The trucks are out of date," Savannah said. "The license tags haven't been renewed."

"Don't these camps try and run cheap?" Leah asked. "Maybe they are just tight."

"Could be," Savannah said. "It feels like more. They wouldn't let all of them go and they wouldn't let them go for this long. Something's not right here. Look at the trucks that have tires instead of tracks, most of the tires are flat...no one has been at this camp for a long time. This place has been abandoned."

"Why would they do that?" Leah asked.

"I don't know," Savannah asked. "Come on, let's check the houses."

Savannah headed over to one of the housing trailers. She took her gun out as she slowly opened the door. As Savannah poked her head in the door, she almost vomited. The smell of death and decay assaulted Savannah's nostrils. As she looked in the trailer, Savannah saw that every bed had a dead body in it. The bodies were all in very poor condition, obviously being killed years ago. Savannah backed out of the trailer and breathed in the fresh air.

"What's in there?" Leah asked.

"Death," Savannah said. "They're all dead."

"How did they die?" Brandi asked.

"I couldn't tell," Savannah said. "I didn't look very closely, but I could tell there wasn't much left of the bodies. I'd bet they'd been in there for two or three years. Brandi, didn't anyone notice that this many men and this much equipment had gone missing or wasn't being used?"

"I don't know," Brandi said. "I mainly hang out at the beach. I don't hear much about what goes on around the park."

"But these people must have had families," Savannah said. "Someone should have come looking for them. There has to be a reason. I mean, the company must have sent someone out to find out what's going on. There's no way there could be this many people hidden out here."

"I have to see this for myself," Leah said. "I want to see what you're talking about."

Leah walked up to the trailer and opened the door. She opened the door and slowly entered the room. The room had a forest smell to it, like wet pine needles. It was a stale smell that wasn't pleasant, but Leah could tell that at one time it must have smelled nice. Leah looked over the beds and areas in the trailer but didn't see any bodies. She couldn't figure out what Savannah had been talking about. Leah exited the trailer.

"There's nothing in there," Leah said. "There are no bodies."

"What?" Savannah said looking in the trailer again. "Where the hell did they all go? They were just here. What the hell is going on?"

Savannah exited the trailer and looked out over the area. She couldn't figure out what was going on. She wanted to search the equipment, find a vehicle that could get them out of the forest, but she didn't want to leave without her friends. Savannah knew they didn't have much time left.

"We should get back to the others," Savannah said. "This site is a bust. I don't know what to make of it."

"We're going to give up on it just like that?" Leah asked.

"I don't know," Savannah said. "What else can we do here?"

"Search the vehicles," Brandi said. "Check over everything. There might be something here that we could use."

"Okay. Let's check everything, but let's do it quickly."

The group split up and started looking over the various pieces of machinery in the yard. Leah hadn't seen anything like the machines that were sitting there. She'd never been much to pay attention to construction crews or anything else that used big equipment. Leah didn't know what to look for as she climbed on the equipment, poking her head in the cabs looking for keys so they could drive one or anything else that would help them.

One by one, Leah searched the machines. She noted that none of them had keys and they were devoid of any supplies. After searching for over twenty minutes, Leah decided to see if the others had found anything yet. Leah walked over by where she'd last seen Savannah and Brandi, but they weren't there. Leah looked around the buildings, but didn't see them. She realized how quiet it had gotten.

"Savannah!" Leah shouted. "Where are you?" There was no reply, only a gentle breeze moving through the trees. Leah ran around the camp, trying to be careful not to injure herself on all the stuff lying around. Leah couldn't see any sign of them. She climbed up a tall piece of machinery and stood on the top to look around.

"Savannah!" Leah shouted again. "Please! Where are you?" Again, there was nothing. Leah threw her hands up in frustration and reached for a flask that wasn't there. She remembered that she'd taken it off and didn't have time to grab it when they'd fled the town. She wondered if it would be best to run back to the other site or to stay and try to find Savannah.

Leah climbed down and made a quick run around the camp. There was no movement, no people anywhere. Leah stopped when she realized that there were shadows in the trees that were moving around. She looked out at them, but none would come far enough into the moonlight so that she could make them out. Leah wanted to shout out for Savannah again, but she didn't dare with the shadows.

As Leah watched the shadows, she saw another figure moving in the woods. It was defiantly a man and as Leah watched she realized that there were two figures moving by the trees. They were trying to avoid the shadows as they moved into the moonlight. Leah breathed a sigh of relief when she saw Todd and Greg's face in the light. Leah ran up to them.

"Am I glad to see you two!" Leah said. "What the hell happened to you guys?"

"We've been attacked," Todd said. "You have to get out of here. What are you doing here? Why did you come here?"

"Jennifer had to find Mike," Leah said. "Where is he? Where's Steve?"

"Things haven't been good," Greg said. "So much has happened since we got out here. You wouldn't believe the things that have happened."

"Do those amazing things include girls showing up at your camp?" Leah asked. "Some younger girls?"

"Two girls showed up," Greg said. "We knew they were young and we told them to leave but they wouldn't. They seemed really weird, something was wrong with them. It didn't take long before they turned on us."

"Was that before or after they took their tops off?" Leah asked.

"They were dead," Todd said. "They were ghosts."

"Yeah right," Leah said. "I've heard you guys say some pretty big lies to justify your partying, but come on, ghosts?"

"You've seen things out here though," Todd said. "You know that we're not alone out here. They were being led by a vicious girl named Melanie. She's the one that's leading all of them. You don't want to mess with her."

"Melanie?" Leah said. "A tan girl with black hair?"

"And too much makeup," Greg said. "She's evil. You have no idea how evil she really is. She tricked all of us, made us separate from the rest of the group. We were captured and placed in a cave not too far from here. We don't know what happened to Mike or Steve. They weren't there. Melanie tortured us. She just wants to hurt people."

"How did you escape?" Leah asked.

"Melanie hasn't been there for about a day," Todd said. "We worked our way out of there. We were tied up, but she didn't tie very good knots. This was the first site we came to once we got out. We wanted to get to the town. There's an abandoned town nearby."

"It's about two miles," Leah said. "We were just there—Jennifer, Roxy, Heidi, Savannah, and I. There have been some strange things going on there too."

"We must do something," Greg said. "We don't have much time."

"We have to get out of this forest," Leah said. "We should run out of the forest to the park rangers and have them send people back up the hills to find the rest."

"Our friends will be dead by then," Greg said. "And everyone we send back will be slaughtered. We have to save all of them now before it's too late."

"What do you suggest we do?" Leah said. "Melanie is at the town hall with the others sleeping right now. How are we supposed to get them out without alerting Melanie?"

"Our only chance is to alert Melanie to what's going on," Greg said. "Someone will have to keep her distracted while the others escape. How could we do that?"

"I have a plan," Todd said. "Let's get back there as quickly as we can."

"We need to find Savannah and Brandi," Leah said. "They were here with me, but I can't find them anymore."

"Brandi?" Greg asked. "The lifeguard from the beach?"

"Yes," Leah replied.

"She's one of them," Todd said. "She's dead, just like they are."

"Impossible," Leah said. "I was just with her and she seemed fine."

"She's a ghost," Todd said. "We need to move now. If Brandi hears our plans she'll do everything she can to stop up from leaving. There's no time to debate about this. Leah, do you know the way back to the town?"

"I do," Leah said. "I still don't feel right about leaving Savannah though."

"She's mostly likely dead by now," Todd said. "We have to go now."

Leah nodded before she slowly started walking towards the trail that they had entered on. Once they got on the actual trail Leah started running with the guys staying just one pace behind her. Leah had always been in good shape but she'd just made this run, it was hot, and she hadn't eaten or drank properly recently. The more they ran the worse Leah felt. She knew there was still a long ways to go and once they met up with the others they'd have to run again, but Leah pushed herself.

As they were running, Leah noticed the shadows in the trees following them throughout the forest. No matter how Leah tried to look at them she could never see their faces, only shadow outlines of what was there. Leah tried to push the image out of her mind as she ran harder. She never bothered to check that the guys were still behind her.

After what seemed like a lifetime of running, Leah broke through the tree line and into the town. The town was still quiet, with nothing moving. Leah raced to the town hall, looking to where Jennifer, Roxy, and Heidi had been, but the girls were no longer there. Leah rushed into the building and to the jail but there was still no sign of her friends. Leah turned around but the guys were gone and only Melanie was standing behind her, blocking the exit out of the room.

"What's going on?" Leah asked. "Where did everyone go?"

"You haven't figured it out yet?" Melanie asked. "You didn't put the pieces together?"

"You're dead," Leah said. "Because you were so dumb and couldn't see through the man you married, you destroyed the town."

"They deserved to be destroyed," Melanie said. "They didn't deserve to live after the way they mocked me, called me a child. I did what I had to do. I was married and had a husband."

"And you brought destruction upon the town that raised you up," Leah said. "You destroyed everyone and everything you knew just to prove that you were an adult? That sounds pretty childish to me. Sounds down right like a baby to me."

"See it your way," Melanie said. "You're not getting out of here alive."

"What did you do to everyone?" Leah asked. "Why do you kill?"

"I kill because I can," Melanie said. "Part of my agreement when I got married. I have to do what my husband says and he likes to kill, even though he denies it now. I like to kill too."

"Who was he?" Leah asked.

"He lived here before the town came about," Melanie said. "They stole his land and his family. They killed them as a warning for him to stay away. They found a shaman who placed a curse so he couldn't come into the town unless he was invited. He found me, gave me what I wanted, and I invited him into the town. That's when we started killing."

"So you kill everyone," Leah said. "You're not killing me." Leah rushed like she was going to get out of the room, but Melanie pulled out a gun, an old flintlock pistol, and shot Leah in the heart as she was almost to her. Leah's eyes got big as she looked down at the cascade of blood that was pouring out of her chest and down her stomach. Leah tried to speak, but nothing came out as she fell to the ground, dead.

"One girl left," Melanie said as she put the gun down. "Oh Savannah, I'm going to enjoy destroying you."

Chapter 19

Savannah looked over the equipment scattered around the camp as she tried to push the shadows watching her out of her mind. The more they moved around, however, the more Savannah noticed them. She climbed into the cab of a massive semi-tractor that had a sleeper on the cab. All the tires on the truck were flat and there was no key. Savannah hit the steering wheel in frustration before looking in the sleeper. It was empty. She was hoping for a vehicle that they could leave the forest in.

Savannah exited the tractor and walked around the trailer. It was a flatbed for hauling logs. Savannah climbed onto the bed to get a better look around. What was bothering her the most was the stunning lack of clues as to what was happening. As Savannah looked around she saw more shadows in the trees but also a small walking trail that led north, further into the hills. She wondered what would be on that trail.

Savannah jumped off the trailer and rushed over to the trail. She investigated the trail as best as she could in the moonlight. Savannah's heart jumped for joy when in the dirt she noticed four distinct shoeprints, the prints that matched the guy's. Savannah could tell that the prints were fairly fresh and they all went in the same direction.

Savannah rushed back into the camp to find Leah and Brandi. She looked around and didn't notice them right away. Savannah began to worry until she rushed around a corner and saw the pair looking over a pickup truck. Savannah rushed up to them.

"Find anything?" Savannah asked.

"Nothing really," Leah said. "You?"

"I did," Savannah said. "There's a walking trail that leads higher into the hills. I saw the guy's shoeprints at the head of the trail."

"You sure it theirs?" Brandi asked. "Could it be from the loggers that were here before?"

"The prints are not more than two days old," Savannah said. "I guarantee it. I think we should go up the trail and see where it takes us."

"Lead the way then," Leah said.

"Brandi," Savannah said. "Do you know where that trail leads to? Have you ever seen a map of this area?"

"No," Brandi replied. "Your guess is as good as mine, but if there's prints there we shouldn't waste any time." Savannah nodded and took off running with the others behind her. The trail was narrow and winding, with steep inclines and declines. It was hard running, but Savannah was able to follow the footprints. The trail was soft dirt that was perfect for tracking. Savannah pushed the others harder and harder as they rushed over the difficult terrain.

The trail rounded a corner before ending in the trees. It was like the trail just stopped in the wall of trees. Savannah came to a stop and looked around. There wasn't enough moonlight coming through the trees for her to read the ground. The ground was covered with an undergrowth that made searching for prints a moot point. Savannah began looking for broken twigs, bent grass, anything that would indicate a direction that the guys went, but there wasn't anything to indicate where they went.

Savannah stood up and looked around the area in the dim moonlight. Brandi and Leah were back a few paces trying to catch their breath. Savannah looked into the trees, trying to find anything that would help them. From the corner of her eyes Savannah thought she noticed something glowing. Savannah, with her gun drawn, walked towards the glowing. As she got closer, she realized that it was coming from a small cave.

The cave was set into the hill and appeared to slope downwards. The opening of the cave was small, barely big enough for a person to slip through. Savannah got close to the entrance she could see that a fire burning. It looked to be surrounded by a makeshift rock fire pit.

"Hello?" Savannah called out. "Is there anybody in there? It's Savannah and Leah. We're here to help you."

"Savannah?" a male voice called out.

"Mike!" Savannah shouted, instantly recognizing the voice. "We're here to rescue you."

Slowly, Mike, Todd, Greg, and Steve made their way out of the cave. The guys were dirty and looked beaten up. They were all wearing shorts and shoes, none of them had tops on. Each guy had scrapes, cuts, and bruises on their exposed upper bodies. Savannah winced when she saw them. They were in a lot of pain. Savannah rushed up and gently hugged them.

"We were so worried about you," Savannah said. "What happened to you?"

"We got lost," Mike said. "It wasn't good."

Leah rushed up and hugged the guys. She gave Greg a kiss on the cheek. "We're just so glad that you're safe," Leah said.

"So it's just you two here for us?" Mike asked.

"Jennifer, Roxy, and Heidi are here too," Savannah said. "There's an abandoned town not far from here. That's where they are at."

"Thank God," Mike said. "We'd set up camp and these girls showed up. We told them to leave, but they wanted to have some fun. We let them drink a little, but nothing else happened. When we went to bed, they stole all our stuff. We had no supplies and couldn't find our way out. We've been wandering since Sunday morning."

"Follow me," Savannah said. "You're safe now."

Savannah took off running, but quickly slowed down when she realized that the guys were in far rougher shape than she'd thought. Savannah kept them at a quick jog. As they moved along, Savannah kept looking back to make sure that all the guys were still hanging with her. There were shadows in the woods, back in the trees, but they seemed to be leaving the group alone. Savannah couldn't wait for Jennifer to see Mike again. She knew it would be a great reunion.

As they entered the town, Savannah took the quickest route over to where the women had been. They were sitting around a small fire with Melanie. Savannah didn't announce them right away, but ran towards them. When the girls realized someone was coming they turned and looked. Jennifer's face lit up when she saw Mike. She rushed to him and when the pair met, they fell to the ground in an embrace.

"Mike!" Jennifer said kissing him. "I was so worried."

"I was afraid that I wouldn't see you again," Mike said. "I love you. You were all I was thinking about Jennifer. I couldn't leave you. The thought of you is what kept me going."

"I love you too," Jennifer said.

"I'll love you forever and for always." Mike and Jennifer got off the ground as the others hugged and exchanged pleasantries for finding the guys. Everyone was tired and ready for this ordeal to be over. Savannah couldn't help but notice that Roxy was sweating heavily.

"Roxy," Savannah asked. "Are you okay?"

"I'm so hot," Roxy said. "God, it's like I'm by a fire or something. I can't figure it out."

"Strange," Heidi said. "I feel like something is around my neck. I've got this weird rope burn that I don't remember how I got."

"I have a weird feeling too," Jennifer said. "My heart."

"That's because I'm back, baby," Mike said with a sly grin.

"No," Jennifer said rubbing her chest. "It's like something's stabbing my heart. I can't explain it."

"I have a similar feeling," Leah said. "But mines a sharp pain right in the heart. Savannah, you feel anything strange?"

"Not really," Savannah said. "What about you guys?"

"I have a strange feeling," Mike said. "Like I'm being held underwater. I feel like something is pulling me down."

"I feel a burning in my stomach," Todd said.

"Same with me," Greg said. "The only thing I can compare it to is the time I accidently drank some poison when I was little."

"I have a massive headache," Steve said. "It feels horrible, like the time I got slammed on the side of my head in a wrestling match. There's so much pain there right now."

"Once we get out of this forest," Savannah said. "Then everything can be taken care of. We did it though. We hiked the hidden trails."

"Don't you think it would be wise to wait until morning?" Melanie asked.

"No," Savannah said. "We need to get out of here right now. There's no time to spare."

"Savannah, please," Mike said. "We haven't had any food in a day or so. We need to eat. We didn't get any sleep in the cave. We were so worried about what was going on. Is there anything to eat here?"

"I can get some more fish," Melanie said. "And there's enough water to share."

"I know you're hungry," Savannah said. "But we should get out of these woods. It's not that far of a hike, only a few hours and we can be back at the park. They have some food there and I'm sure we can eat. I'm sure that police and park rangers are out looking for us."

"Savannah," Leah said. "Why don't you use the radio? See if they can come up here and get us? That would be a lot faster."

"But then they would know we found the hidden trails," Savannah said. "We can walk out and we should walk out right now, before anything else happens."

"We have to let them eat," Jennifer said. "They can eat quickly then we can get out of here. We all need to get home and get cleaned up."

Savannah nodded, realizing she was outnumbered. She knew they needed to leave, but the guys wanted to eat. The group quickly prepared a light meal of fish and some fruit. The women gave the guys the last of the beef jerky and trail mix. Savannah paced the entire time the guys were eating, hoping that they would hurry up. Once they were done, Savannah rallied everyone together.

"Okay," Savannah said. "We all need to stay close together and keep your eyes on the person in front of you. We cannot get separated out here."

"Melanie," Leah asked. "Are you coming with us? You could come out with us."

"I'm staying," Melanie said. "This place is my home now. Amber Hollow is my home. I hope that you decide to come back and visit me sometime. I would really love to have visitors."

"We'll be back," Leah said. "I promise you that."

"Right," Savannah said. "Let's move out."

Savannah led the group as they raced through the forest. The guys seemed to be doing better now that they'd eaten. The group moved quickly as they raced down the hills. Savannah hoped they could get to the park before daylight and be able to leave before all the rangers and police were up. She figured that if they could get out of there, then the questioning later on would be much easier.

The girls passed a smaller site along the river and Savannah couldn't help but notice something. She wasn't sure what she saw but something told her that she need to stop and see what was there. Savannah stopped the group and got them all together.

"Hold here for a second," Savannah said. "I need to check something."

Savannah walked over by the river and looked around. She could feel that something was out of place, but she didn't realize what it was right away. That's when she saw it; a body was tied to a tree. Savannah walked over to the body and her heart almost stopped when she saw the face of the body; Brandi. Savannah knew that Brandi was running with them. She couldn't figure out how this could be possible. There was no obvious reason as to how Brandi died, but she was dead and tied to this tree even though she was standing only a few feet away from Savannah. Savannah walked back to the group.

"What was it?" Jennifer asked.

"Must have been an animal or something," Savannah said. "It couldn't have been anything. I mean, I didn't see anything over there."

"Then we need to keep moving," Jennifer said.

Savannah nodded and took off running. The group, including Brandi, followed her. Savannah couldn't even begin to explain what was going on, she just wanted to get out of the woods. Savannah knew that once she got to the park, the rangers or the police could help them. Savannah ran faster, letting the others fall behind. Even the guys were having trouble keeping up with her as she ran.

They passed everything without stopping. The logging site, the campsite, all the little stops that they made along the way. All Savannah wanted to do was get back to the park. She knew that they had to be very close. She was almost exhausted when Mike tripped on his feet and hit the ground. The entire group stopped and tried to help him up.

"What's wrong?" Savannah asked.

"We can't keep up," Mike said. "We need to have a break."

"He's right, Savannah," Roxy said. "None of us are in as good of shape as you are. We need to rest for a few minutes."

"We can't be that far from the park," Jennifer said. "Savannah, run ahead and get food and water ready for us when we get there."

"We can't let them know," Savannah said. "We need to slip out silently and let them know we got home safe."

"Why?" Jennifer asked.

"That way we don't have to answer questions," Savannah said. "We can get out of here so we don't have to tell them where we were."

"Please Savannah," Mike said. "We need help. They will find out anyway. We won't be in that much trouble. We are willing to face the music. We just need help."

"Just go ahead and get stuff ready for us," Jennifer said. "You are the only one who's still healthy enough to do this."

"Okay," Savannah said. "Stay on this trail and don't wander. Don't wait too long either; we need to get home. I told you I'd get you home Jennifer. I promised all of you that I would save you and I did. We made it."

Savannah took a last look at her friends before she started running again. Savannah raced as fast as she could to get to the park. When she finally entered the main trailhead, Savannah wanted to shout with joy. She was so happy she could barely contain herself. Savannah rushed to a cabin that was near the ranger station and began pounding on her door.

After a moment the door opened and Lacey, tired and in her pajamas, stood in the doorway. She seemed very confused to see Savannah standing there.

"Savannah," Lacey said. "We were worried about you. We hadn't seen a trace of you or the guys for some time now."

"They are safe now," Savannah said. "They are back up the trail and on their way here. They're in rough shape. We need to get food and water ready to go when they arrive here."

"Where did everyone go?" Lacey said. "Where were they? We searched everywhere."

"They had gotten on the hidden trails," Savannah said. "We hiked up to Amber Hollow and saw an abandoned logging camp that was only a mile or so away. What happened to that logging camp?"

"They met with what destroyed the town of Amber Hollow," Lacey said stepping out of the way and ushering Savannah into the cabin. "Come in, you look horrible."

Savannah entered the cabin and Lacey shut the door. Savannah followed Lacey to a table. Savannah sat down while Lacey got her something to eat. Lacey handed her some deli meats, fresh fruit, and a glass of water. Savannah devoured the food quickly.

"That was good," Savannah said. "Thank you."

"Not a problem," Lacey said.

"So what destroyed Amber Hollow?" Savannah asked. "What happened up there?"

"It's a long story, Savannah," Lacey said. "I hate to tell it. Did you meet a girl named Melanie?"

"Yes, we did," Savannah said.

"She died a long time ago," Lacey said flatly. "When she met a man who tricked her. The man had been banned from the town and needed an invitation to get in, Melanie gave him that invitation. They killed for a few years until those left in the town left. Now she loves playing with people. She loves killing them. It's a cat and mouse game to her. She loves to torment people as she does it, playing games with them."

"I don't believe you," Savannah said.

"You saw the shadows in the trees?" Lacey asked.

"Yes."

"They're her dead," Lacey said. "Those that died by Melanie's hand."

"What happened to her husband?" Savannah asked. "Why does Melanie do all the killing? What does he do?"

"All he wanted was revenge against Amber Hollow," Lacey said. "He was banned from the town for practicing sorcery."

"What about us?" Savannah asked. "What about my friends?"

"They're all dead," Lacey said. "Heidi was hung. Roxy was burned. Jennifer was stabbed.

Leah was shot. Mike was drowned. Steve was hit on the head. Todd and Greg were poisoned."

"The girls who were in the tent with them?" Savannah asked. "The tops that we found?"

"Todd and Greg had a lot of fun with those girls," Lacey said. "But they had been dead for a long time. They were ghosts. Melanie lets some of the people play with her. They were the big figures you saw the first night and were the ones that took the other tents away. They can change their forms somewhat."

"Why are you telling me this?" Savannah asked. "What happens now? I don't believe you that everyone is dead."

"They are Savannah," Lacey said. "Brandi's dead too. You saw the body."

"I did," Savannah said. "And I spoke to Brandi after I saw her dead body tied to a tree. Are you dead too?"

"No," Lacey said.

As Savannah was about to ask a question, Melanie and a tall and lank man, with a handlebar mustache walked into the room. They held hands.

Savannah instantly realized that he was the man who'd warned them off when they started.

"I had a feeling about you Savannah," Melanie said. "I thought you would make it back. You survived, so I'm not going to kill you, but you cannot leave. You can never leave this park."

"Why not?" Savannah asked. "Why did your husband warn us? Doesn't he want to kill?"

"He'd rather not kill...anymore...so he tries to warn people. It's not very effective though," Melanie said. "If you leave the park or tell anyone about what you've seen here, I will kill you after I force you to watch each of your friends deaths over and over again, understand?"

"I do," Savannah said. "Kill me now and get it over with."

"I'm not going to do that," Melanie said. "You will behave or else." Melanie's husband flicked his wrist and Savannah was on the ground, screaming and writhing in pain. The pain was so great she could barely stand it. As quickly as the pain started, it stopped. He flicked his wrist again and Savannah's clothes morphed into a red, one-piece lifeguard swimsuit. Savannah slowly stood and looked at it.

"Brandi died," Melanie said. "You're the new lifeguard for the park. Get used to the job. You're quitting school and turning your job offer down. You're working here from now on. I like you though. You're a tough girl, big and strong. You'll need to keep that up. If anyone talks about the trails, if anyone wants to know about them, you play dumb. We want people to find it, we like having visitors. I hope you enjoy your new life."

Melanie and her husband walked out of the cabin leaving Savannah and Lacey alone. Savannah tried to process everything that had just happened. She'd never believed in ghosts before, but now all her friends were left in the forest as ghosts. Savannah didn't understand.

"Just do as she says," Lacey said. "Morris entered Amber Hollow twenty years ago, I entered over thirty years ago. Melanie will keep you looking young. Had Morris and I knew that's where the guys were headed, we would have stopped them. We try to destroy all the places that know about the trails. We try to keep people safe. Sorry."

"Are there any benefits to being like this?" Savannah asked.

"You can't get pregnant," Lacey said. "All the sex you want and you don't have to worry about disease or getting knocked up. You get food and a roof over your head. All the booze you can drink."

"But we can't leave," Savannah said.

"There are worse things that could happen," Lacey said standing. "Far worse things could happen. It's just about light out. You need to get to the beach and get things ready to go for the morning. Trust me Savannah, it may seem unfair or cruel, but you will understand and come to enjoy this. You will have a decent life here, but you cannot leave. Remember that if you try to leave, Melanie will have us hunt you down and bring you back. Then, you'll most likely be killed after you're tormented. Things could be far worse though, you're not dead and rotting away in the forest like your friends."

Lacey nodded and walked into a different room in the cabin. Savannah looked down at the suit she was now wearing. She didn't know what happened to her other clothes. Savannah noticed a mirror and looked at herself in it. She'd always hated wearing one piece swimming suits. She thought that if she was forced to be here, she should at least get to wear what she wanted. As she thought about it, her clothing changed to exactly what she was thinking about; a red, lifeguard bikini top and black bikini bottoms. Savannah concentrated again, trying to change her outfit but it didn't work. She tried to add a cover up but that didn't work either. Savannah sighed as she left the cabin.

Savannah slowly made her way to the beach and looked at the sun that was just starting to break over the horizon. She realized that in a twisted way, she'd gotten what she wanted. She never had to deal with her family again and she never had to grow up. After all she'd been through in her life, and all the people who'd come in and out of her life, Savannah realized that she always had one friend who'd never let her down and was always there for her. It was the one friend Savannah realized would always be there no matter what. It was her best friend—the forest.

About the Author

Leif J. Erickson was born and raised on a grain farm outside Wheaton, MN, just a stone's throw from White Rock, SD, which served as the inspiration for the Ghost Town series. From a very early age, Leif knew that he was going to be a farmer, just like his father and grandfather. As he grew up, Leif learned everything he could about farming, always riding in equipment with his dad and helping out wherever he could.

After Leif graduated high school he attended North Dakota State University in Fargo, North Dakota, where he achieved a BS in Agricultural Economics along with a minor in History. During his time in college, Leif networked with many other farmers from across North Dakota, South Dakota, and Minnesota, while advancing his knowledge in all aspects of agricultural. With a diploma in hand, Leif returned to the family farm and started his career as a farmer.

The first season was very successful and stood as a testament to the hard work and education that Leif had received. All signs pointed to a lifetime career as a farmer until a family tragedy struck and the family farm was dispersed. For the first time in his life, Leif didn't know what he wanted to pursue for a career.

Leif returned to Fargo, ND where he began his career as a stock and futures trader. It was during this time that he began to become serious about writing. With one computer watching the markets, Leif would be on the other, writing. Leif quickly realized though that Fargo wasn't the city or location that he wanted to make a home in. Less than one year since he moved there, Leif moved to Plymouth MN, in the Twins Cities area.

Continuing with the trading and writing, Leif began to learn everything that he could about writing, about storytelling, and about the hero's journey. Leif spent his spare time reading novels or books about writing. It was during his time in the Cities that Leif wrote many, many different stories, getting the outlines and first drafts finished. In the three years that Leif was in the Cities, he wrote the first draft for over fifty different stories.

Leif received information about a career opportunity that was back in his hometown of

Wheaton so he returned to go to work for the local grain elevator. The work was hard and the days were long without much time for writing. Leif missed being able to write every day. He had so many more stories that he wanted to write. Being aggressive and a hard worker, Leif quickly moved up the ladder in the company and within six months he was in a management position.

Although Leif had met and dated many women when he was in the Twin Cities, it was in Wheaton where he met the new Science Teacher at his old High School and within fifteen months of meeting the pair were married at Good Shepherd Lutheran Church in Wheaton. Many have described the pair as absolutely made for each other, and they spend much of their time hiking in State Parks or canoeing the local lakes and rivers.

Being back in Wheaton, Leif used his free time to polish up and finish some of his stories. He got two stories to the point where he was satisfied to bring them to the marketplace and share them with others. Although he still works for the elevator, Leif looks forward to the day when he can write fulltime, offering more novels and screenplays to entertain and delight others.

During his life, Leif was always quick to be able to tell a story. He had an uncanny ability to quickly make up a story on the spot (sometimes to the dismay of parents and teachers) and to pull people into the story with wild characters, amazing locations, and fantastical storylines. Although Leif focuses on science fiction, he's written stories in many different genera's including mystery, horror, teen comedy, western, and even a little romance.

Throughout Leif's writings you can see traces of his farm life and his love of nature. Being an ecologist and former farmer, much of Leif's writings feature forests, lakes, and nature in general. Leif has always been interested in science and what's possible for the human race, pushing the envelope of technologies, and finding how far humans can go. Much of Leif's science fiction writing explores these themes and ideas.

When he's not writing, Leif and his wife Brittany can be found working on their goal of hiking in every State Park in Minnesota or on the lakes and rivers in a canoe. The pair have some big canoe adventures planned, and have already canoed, from end to end, big lakes such as Lake Traverse and Big Stone Lake. Every once in a while, Leif will pull out his old Disc Jockey system and play a dance as the 'Leif of the Party DJ Service.'

Leif has been influenced by many different writers and stories. His all-time favorite story is 'Sleepy Hollow' by Washington Irving, a story that Leif reads every Halloween. Other influences on his work are the 'Dune' series by Frank Herbert, 'The Lord of the Rings' by J.R.R. Tolkien, and anything related to the Arthurian Legend. Leif also enjoys many other authors such as Charles Dickens, Michael Crichton, John Steinbeck, Isaac Asimov, Neil Gaiman, and F. Scott Fitzgerald just to name a few. Thank you for checking out a book by Leif Erickson. Please visit his website at www.leifericksonwriting.com and purchase the other books that Leif has written. They will take you on a journey that you will never forget...